Doctor Mooze

Published by bluechrome publishing

bluechrome publishing, PO Box 109, Portishead, Bristol BS20 7ZJ

First Edition 2003
Revised, Second Edition Published by bluechrome 2007

A CIP catalogue record for this book is
available from the British Library

www.bluechrome.co.uk
www.erikryman.co.uk

ISBN 978-1-906061-04-3

Illustrations are by Sean Michael O'Brien, aged 11.

Printed by Biddles Ltd, King's Lynn, Norfolk

Doctor Mooze

Erik Ryman

also by Erik Ryman

the tsetsefly chronicles
God's Game

Introduction

Doctor Mooze was originally meant to be a short story, something that could be read to my then unborn son but, as with most things in life, it was not quite that simple. Instead it became the final diary of a ten-year-old boy, Panton di Villa, and was published in his name...and man was he a brat.

Reviewers loved it, hated it, and weren't sure whether it was true or not. Too neat to be true, I think, was the general opinion - although no-one was really sure.

Which of course was the original intent.

But that was then, and as it is being reissued I thought I'd better come clean. At least this way Jack gets his dedication, even if it will be a while before I let him read it.

Erik Victor Ryman
Spring 2007

for Jack

Saturday 21st December

Hi! Welcome to my blog. I'm going to be writing it every day from now on until it gets really big. Then I'll sell advertising on it so millions of people read it.

OK, it's not on the internet yet, cos I haven't got round to learning how to do that, but I've got a copy of Word my Dad lifted from work and I know how to use it. I thought I'd wait 'til I've got a bit more and it's worth the effort. I can't see the point in learning how to do all that shit and then getting bored with writing this and it's all a waste - I mean, who's going to pay for advertising if there's only one or two pages?

Cool. I've done half a page already and it ain't *sooo* very hard. Man, that *sbentter* Matthews - he's in my class and he's been trying to do a blog for months and all he's got on it is stuff about his holiday in Portugal. Some of the pictures of women were cool – his Dad had done this sneaky thing where he took photos of Matthews' Mum on an air bed - well stupid she looked - and had made sure that there were these real cool girls in the background. Matthews used Coral Picture to cut his Mum out and put a pic of himself in the middle so it looked like these cool girls were checking him out. They looked German – well my brother Toto said so and he knows cos he's got these magazines hidden in his bedroom. It was *sooo* funny the other day when Mum started tidying his room, and he had to try and get her out. It was *sooo* cool, cos me and Toto were saying 'Hey Mum, there's someone at the door'. Then Toto said that he'd broken his foot and started hopping around and stuff like a real *nonno*. I was laughing, and Mum kept telling him to stop 'trying to be clever' which made me laugh even more cos he just looked *sooo* very stupid.

My blog's going to be about real things. I'm on my second page now and haven't even said what it is I like to do. Oh man, this is going to be easy. Maybe I *will* learn that internet stuff so people can see it.

I'm going to shoot some rabbits now with Dad. We've got a problem with vermin and we're willing to take a responsible approach to managing it. That's what he told the smelly reporter when those hippy blokes with beards and those ugly women told on him to the papers and the radio people kept coming round to his work and telling lies about him.

We have to kill the rabbits when it's dark now so that no-one can see us and we've got to do it tonight because the man from the fur factory is coming round in the morning and he pays us money for them. My Dad says it's secret, so not to tell anyone, especially not reporters.

Panton

Panton Boarding

Sunday 22nd December

Hi again! Welcome back to my blog. I guess I've got to keep writing every day if I'm going to sell it to someone and get adverts, but I had an awesome day today cos we went to see a football match.

It was really good   not like when you play it on the PS2 and you don't really get involved. You can shout at people and sing songs and stuff. Dad got funny when these people kept singing songs with dirty words – I think he thought we hadn't heard them before. He tried to pretend like he couldn't understand what they were saying, and Toto kept asking him what the words were so he could join in. I think Dad knew that Toto knew and he kept raising his eyebrows in my direction, but Toto kept pretending that he didn't realise. I mean, I'm ten years old and he still thinks I'm a kid or something. Like I don't know how to say 'fuck':

Fuck fuck fuck fuck fuck fuck fuck fuck fuck fuck fuck fuck fuck fuck fuck fuck fuck fuck fuck fuck fuck fuck fuck.

I mean it's not hard is it? Every fucking television show says fuck and we always watch films and things where people say fuck and worse words. He does though - he really does think I'm a kid still.

I guess all Dads are like that - they want to be your best buddy – but when it comes to things that your best buddy wouldn't want you to do, like cleaning and homework and putting your light out when you're on *Havoc Hotel* or something, well then they get to be Dads again and look lame.

Toto says that he could be a Dad if he wanted to, because he's got hair starting to grow on his balls. He's older than me. I'm not sure if I'd want hair on my balls - it looks kind of itchy. I don't know why having balls with hair on them would let you be a Dad either. I know my Dad has got hair on his balls too – I saw them once when we went swimming and shared a changing room.

Once they put a big monster in the middle of the pool, and me and Toto were running from one side of the pool, up the monster's legs, over its body then bombing into the little kids like that blubber belly bloke in the TV advert. That was wicked, but then Dad became a Dad again and stopped us doing it just because some little girl broke her arm or something.

I mean, we didn't hit her or nothing - one of her friends jumped on her, not us. But Dad kept talking about insurance (like so what?) and how lawyers ruled the world and things, and then we had to go.

Toto said that it was Dad who threw the girl's friend into the water and that was why we went, but I don't know – I never saw nothing, cos I'm no grass and he's family is Tony.

Anyway, after the football we went to McDonalds (another thing Dads do when they're in Buddy mode – like calling you 'mate' and trying to chase after you until they run out of breath and start smoking again).

Dad's meant to have stopped smoking, but I saw him outside his office when we went on our school trip on a coach and he was definitely smoking and it was definitely him, you know? I'm keeping that to myself though - cos I ain't no grass and he's, like, family.

I like the Sopranos - we saw them when we stayed at Nan's house. She's my Dad's Mum, my Mum's Mum is dead. I think it was in the war or something, least that's what Toto says and he's older than me. I guess he means the Iraq one that was on when I was born. That was like really cool, like a computer game or something – Dad kept his old videos and we saw it on Fox last Christmas. Dad says there's going to be another war with Iraq and that we've got to do the job right this time. I don't really know what that means cos all the films I saw were wicked and we smashed all those Iraq tanks and things to pieces. I don't know if maybe it took too long or we ran out of time. Toto just laughed at me because I wrote 'run out of lives' like it was a real computer game, not a thing on TV. Toto says that the Americans had a cheat where they always had extra lives, but that they were English lives. I don't get that and he won't explain. Ever since he started getting fur on his balls he's been saying things like that, like I'm stupid or something for not understanding what he's on about, you know? I told him he's getting to be more of a Dad everyday. He ain't talking to me now – and I don't care.

He's started hanging out with Becky Allen as well. He reckons she's his girlfriend, but Becky's sister Kate who's in my class and plays football with us and is like quite cool for a girl – she looks like Avril Lavigne, who did that song, *Skater Boy* – well she said that Toto wants to go out with Becky but that Becky wouldn't let him feel her up or even kiss her with tongues. Kate says Becky's a cockteaser, but she didn't know what it meant when I asked her. I think that's what Toto does sometimes, he uses big words so that he looks cleverer than he really is in front of girls – but I don't reckon he knows what he's talking about.

I think that's the worse thing to be, somebody who pretends to be cleverer than they are just to look cool or something. I just asked my Dad and he reckons you call it a 'Phoney' – like I didn't know that. He said John Lennon (that singer from the old days) got shot because someone thought he was a phoney.

Anyway, gotta go to bed now cos Dad's being a Dad again and still trying to lay that 'Got to be good for Father Christmas' stuff on me.

Oh yeah, The other thing I like did today that was *sooo* cool was to have a look at Toto's magazines – the ones that he has to hide from Mum and Dad cos they've got pictures of German women with no clothes and stuff. Mum would go *sooo* mad if she knew that Toto had them under his bed in this hole he cut in the carpet like the trapdoor under our tree house. You can't see it until you get really close, which is hard cos it's under the bed and you've got to take these big drawers out that are full of games Toto used to play when he was a kid and all – Lego and Meccano and shit. I don't think he ever played with the Meccano, though, cos when Dad gave it to him for Christmas – well we thought it was still Father Christmas then - Dad made Toto sit with him while he made this really big crane that went up and down and swung round. It took my Dad hours and Toto was saying 'Can I have a go?' but my Dad was really into it and just kept saying that Toto should watch so that he could do it himself next time. But once my Dad had finished the crane was *really* big and used nearly every nut and bolt and bit of holey metal and stuff - well he wouldn't let Toto take it apart in case he couldn't put it back together the same. All Toto wanted to do was play and make like a tank or a car or something but in the drawer under the bed it's still like the crane Dad built except Toto bent it all up to fit it in.

Most of the magazines Toto's got are stuck together cos they were wet when he found them in the park and he had to dry them under his bed. They smelt weird and like bleach and they all seem to have crap stories and pictures of women with no clothes or anything. Toto doesn't know that I know they're there, cos it's meant to be some big lame secret and stuff, but I watched him hiding them in his carpet trapdoor once when I was hiding in his wardrobe and he came into the room. I just kept quiet and he shut his bedroom door and pulled this magazine from out of the back of his cargoes and put it under the carpet. I kept really quiet and snuck out when he went to the bathroom to read one of his other magazines. Most of them are really boring, but I do like *FHM* and *GQ* cos they have really interesting stories and things and don't just have pictures of women sticking their lips out like they're gonna cry or something.

Anyway, today was really cool cos I nicked the Christmas *FHM* and *GQ* magazines and hid them in my bedroom under my PS2 games so that I can read about clothes and gadgets and stuff.

My Dad said that he'll take me to buy some cool clothes in the January Sales cos I've got taller and I'm a lot thinner than Toto so I can't wear his old stuff - like I'd want to, right? He said that cos I'm 'taking a serious interest in developing myself via the exciting medium of the World Wide Web he'd like to reward my interest by buying me some of the modern clothing I seem to like.' Toto asked if that meant I was going to get some cool designer clothes and Dad said 'certainly - as long as they're not too dear and will last a while.'

Toto got really pissed off cos all he ever got when he got interested in the internet was this really lame cordless mouse that didn't even work unless you were behind the computer and everything. It doesn't really seem that fair cos Toto knows loads more than me about computers and web stuff and that – but that's Dads isn't it? Mum would have made sure that they spent exactly the same amount of money on both of us so that we don't get jealous or anything, but Dad just says things then looks stupid when it doesn't go quite right.

Panton

Monday 23rd December

Cool. Monday morning and no school. I'm going to try and write every morning now cos Mum is giving me hassle about staying up late and getting black rings under my eyes. Don't hear her saying that to my Dad when he's been drinking beer with Uncle Terry and ends up throwing up everywhere. He isn't really my uncle though - just somebody my Dad works with and goes and plays snooker with on a Friday.

That's something else they do to you when they think you're still a kid, they tell you all their friends are your aunts and uncles when they just ain't, you know? It's like we never did family trees in school did we? It ain't hard is it? – I tried to explain it to Mum. If Terry was her brother or Dad's brother then he'd be my uncle. As he isn't either of them, unless Mum or Dad could have a black brother, which would be hard cos they're both white, then he isn't my uncle.

She just told me to stop being clever like my brother (cos he's *sooo* very clever with his furry balls).

When I was younger (nine I think) I did ask Terry if he was adopted and if that was how come we were related. But he got funny with me and my Dad told me to apologise – don't know why, but he always does. Toto says it's because Terry *is* adopted and doesn't know who his Mum and Dad are – but I think he's just being a phoney again. Mum said it's just a nice thing to say, calling Terry my uncle, and I do quite like him cos he laughs a lot and has lots of teeth. His son is cool too - he's called Minto - but he's 13 and won't talk to me and always fights with Toto, so he's my enemy even though I think I like him.

Toto is 14 by the way. He goes to the same school as me but doesn't talk to me when we're there, cos it isn't really cool to be seen with your little brother. He used to be OK, and I guess he *is* still my best friend even if he's turning into a phoney, but he doesn't want to play with me most of the time anymore. I guess I pissed him off one time too many, or maybe he's just an asshole.

Dad called the man at the garage an asshole, and I quite like that - *asshole.* He says things like that when my Mum isn't around and he's trying to be the cool buddy guy again. Toto laughed and told me that Buddy Guy is a singer who plays guitar and used to play with Elvis (I just found out that Elvis is the one that sang that *Little Less Conversation* song, and that he isn't the black guy who does the cool dancing on the DVD. Elvis was some old fat man who died on the toilet. Toto says that he died about 25 years ago – but how can he have made the song?)

Phoney phoney phoney phoney phoney phoney phoney phoney fuck fuck fuck fuck fuck fuck fuck fuck phoney fuck Toto is a foney phuck foney phuck foney phuck foney phuck

Getting bored with this now, going to go play with my WWE wrestlers. My favourite is the Undertaker who is 6 foot 10 inches tall and has been the WWE Champion 4 times (OK, it used to be called the WWF and I don't think he's won it since it became WWE after the panda people complained that people thought wrestling had something to do with pandas – doh!). He was the WWE Tag Team Champion 6 times and also the Hardcore Champion, but I don't remember that. Oh yeah, he won the WCW Tag Team belt as well, but that's not like a real thing, it's just where the wrestlers go when they either want a rest because they're getting too old or they want to get a new image or something. My wrestlers are action figures, which is pretty cool, but Toto rips it out of me if I play with them when he's around so I tend to hide them in my bedroom until he goes and plays with Becky. Most of my friends play the PS2 game instead, but it isn't the same. Anyway, when I grow up I've decided that if I can't be in a band like *Linkin Park* - cos I can't play guitar or drums or sing or anything and Dad won't buy me lessons or nothing – or if I can't even be in *Wheatus* who Toto said don't even play their own instruments so it wouldn't matter if I couldn't or anything – well I've decided that I'm going to be a dodgy estate agent in London even if it *is* full of foreigners and cockney scummers like Dad says. See, I've been reading in Toto's *GQ* magazine about the Mini Cooper S which is the coolest car ever – even if James Bond uses a BMW or something, cos it has a 1,598cc four cylinder, 16-valve engine and goes really quick doing 0-60 in 7.2 seconds and has a mad top speed of 135 miles per hour. Which wouldn't beat many things in *Top Trumps* or anything, but my Dad says it would feel a lot quicker cos you sit so close to the ground and feel every little bump and stuff like a roller coaster. Like the one in Blackpool where I went with Mum and Uncle Terry when Dad was in France buying cigarettes he doesn't smoke, and I threw up after we went to Pizza Hut and caught that lame bus that has to follow rails and goes really slow along by the sea.

I really like the red Mini with the white stripes on the bonnet and in *GQ* they say that they're going to re-make that old film where the classic really small Minis chase each other around cos they've robbed a bank or something. But they're going to use the new Mini, which is really cool even if it's foreign now, and the engine is made in Brazil and the Government sold off the family silver like Dad says. I don't know what that means but I didn't want him asking me about *GQ* so I left it. Anyway, in *GQ* they said that dodgy estate agents in London have all been given a Mini Cooper S for free even though they normally cost £14,500. I'll write more later if I can think of anything.

Panton

Tuesday 24th December

Hiya again. Tutu (my new name for my brother) has been showing me how to make my own cool logo like Sony have – you know, the circles with the square and triangle in them. If I get a mobile phone for Christmas (I don't think Mum minds cos Tutu has one and she says she feels safer with me having one too, but Dad isn't into the idea, so I'll know tomorrow I guess) - well, if I get one, I wanted the Sony sign as the graphic, but now I want to make my own up.

Tutu just told me that I can't cos you need special computers to do it. Why does he always spoil things?

TuTutuTutuTutuTutu foney phuck TutuTutuTutuTututu is so foney, so foney a foney foney phuck.

Anyway, my logo is cool. Look,

PANTON

OK, it's not exactly the same, but it's got my name on it and Sony don't even have their name on theirs – so mine is better.

I've done one for Tutu as well,

FONEYPHUCK

Actually, today Toto has been really nice and showed me how to do more with the computer and things. It's just, I don't know, you get shown these things at school but they only ever show you the really boring things like Excel and Word and things and then you're allowed to go on to really boring web sites that are meant to teach you things. I mean, why is it that all things you do at school are *sooo* boring?

We had to play this car game at school and everyone was talking about how we're going to play this really cool driving game and we're all thinking it's going to be wicked, cos car games usually are and we're all imagining *Grand Theft Auto III* or something and when we sit down at the computers the game is shit. Fucking shit. I mean they're all so foney – foney phucks. If you're going to get a game that's meant to teach you something, why does it have to be such a shit game? Couldn't we have a good game that we like playing, I mean if it's good for you why does it have to be shit? I mean this car game, right - it didn't even have a car in it! All you did was drive letters around the screen to make words up – it was like reception class. I told my Dad and he said it's because educationalists teach because they cannot do, and there are obviously educationalist computer programmers who put these games together. Toto said he means that shit programmers write shit games and only teachers would be stupid enough to buy them

Anyway, I've had such a cool time with Toto on the computer today. As well as showing me how to do logos, he showed me how to use a program called *Photoshop*. I think it must be another one my Dad got from work, and I didn't really understand it all, but it has this wicked tool that lets you turn pictures into water (Tutu says liquefy) and make them look weird.

I got a picture of Ms Courtney, my English teacher, and made her look really weird. My Dad says she looks like Cherie Blair now. Toto has just shown me how to put a picture in Word - this is really cool!

Mum has just told us off for playing with Ms Courtney's picture. She was more angry with Dad though, cos she'd told him to throw away the school calendar we scanned the picture off. Toto thinks it's really funny, cos he's been saying for ages that Dad fancied her and that's why the calendar was on June for six months. Ms Courtney smokes as well, I think that's why Mum doesn't like her.

Mum's got this thing about smoking cos her brother died because he used to smoke a lot and got a cancer that made his hair fall out and made him look really grey and he got thin really quickly. Dad told us that he wasn't well and that we shouldn't smoke cigarettes, cos they're bad for you. Mum told us that they're really expensive in England and that Dad only used to smoke because they were cheap when he grew up in Spain, but that in England you might as well roll up a five-pound note and burn it. Yeah right – cos you'd do that – doh! I know Toto smokes sometimes and I worry that he's going to get cancer and his hair will fall out, though he always has it short anyway so I guess it wouldn't matter much, and anyway he's a bit fatter than me so it might be good for him. Mum's always trying to lose weight, but I wouldn't dare tell her she should smoke – she hates it that much. Toto says that cigarettes make you cool, but I think they just make you smell bad.

Well, tomorrow is Christmas and Mum just told me that I should be making Christmas cards on the computer, not writing my silly blog. Shows how much she knows – I did the cards already (OK Toto helped me, but I messed with the pictures) and all I've got to do is print them and I've finished. Easypeasy.

Toto was really nice today, not a foneyphuck. I think it was because he hasn't seen Becky Allen and he doesn't have to pretend he's clever.

Panton

Wednesday 25th December

******** It's Christmas! ********

Hiya, Dad said I could write some more of my blog while him and Mum go for a sleep. I think they've had too much turkey or something, because they both keep burping and things. Dad said I could go on the computer on my own cos Toto has gone to give Becky a Christmas present he bought from his pocket money. Mum thinks he's really sweet now, but she doesn't know that he'd spent his pocket money on cigarettes and that he got the money for Becky's present from her purse. I told him she'll kill him if she finds out and he promised to help me use a chat room if I didn't tell her. I didn't tell him that I wouldn't anyway. I mean, I ain't no grass.

Well I got my mobile fone, but it hasn't got the Wheatus ring tone on it. Toto said he would help me find some free ones on the internet when he gets back. The fone I got is a Saygem myG-5, which is a pay-as-you-go fone with an Orange tariff. It's really cool cos it's totally set up for playing games. It is the *exact* one I wanted and comes with special gaming features (I haven't found out what they are yet, but the buttons look kind of like a PS1 controller, though I don't think it will have rumble on it), polyphonic ring tones which Dad said means it's real music not just one note at a time, and a colour screen which is really bright. It's just *sooo* wicked. Best of all it comes with free SMS messages for 3 whole months. I can also use it to go on the internet but Toto says it's 'Wap' which is German for 'crap' and that it's just a waste of money. I'll try it though, just not when he's hanging around, I guess. I want to get a Linkin Park cover for it next, but I think they cost a lot of money.

Other presents I got were a miniature digital camera from Toto that hangs from a key ring on your belt. He says that you can plug it into our computer and then play with the pictures in

Photoshop, but that Dad will have to try and get a lead from work cos the camera hasn't got one. I think it's because he stole the camera from the Gadget Shop when we went to Bristol Christmas shopping, but Mum thinks he bought it.

Uncle Terry got me a drum that's covered in this really bright coloured cloth with lots of beads. I don't think Dad liked it when Toto and me were pretending to be those blokes from the advert who play the dustbins. Mum said it was a lovely present and that we'd have to write Terry a thank you letter. I think Mum likes Terry like Dad likes Ms Courtney, cos she always seems to act funny when he's in our house and plays with her hair.

The other present I got was a book from Minto – well not really from Minto, cos his Mum always buys us the present from him and our Mum buys him a present from us. It's all foney, but the present I got was cool, cos it's a book called *The Worst Case Scenario: Survival Guide* and it had loads of really cool information about how you can escape from quicksand or deliver a baby in a taxi or take a punch and things. There's also a really cool website that lets you email people really funny stuff, like a letter you can use to dump your girlfriend.

Anyway, Toto told us all during dinner that he'd had a wet dream. Mum sent him upstairs and Dad went to have a serious talk with him. I was going to ask Mum what it meant, but she just looked at me and said 'No'. I know that voice, it's the one she used to talk to Dad about the school calendar and he didn't argue with her either. I'll ask Toto when he gets back

I also got a book about using computerss off Dad and Mum, but why would I read about it when Toto can show me? That makes sense – doh!

It is nice to get presents from Mum and Dad though. When I was younger and didn't know that Father Christmas didn't exist (Toto told me to see if I would cry and I did), I was always sad because I thought that Mum and Dad didn't buy us any Christmas presents even though everybody else did.

Anyway, I'm going to write my thank you letters now.

Panton

Thursday 26th December

Hiya. Dad just told me that Boxing Day is the shittiest day of the year as all you get is a hangover and gut-rot from the turkey. I don't think that's totally true cos Toto has just come back from Becky's house and he's got a love bite all over his neck.

I couldn't stop laughing - even Mum was asking him if they have food in their house. Dad started trying to find garlic to keep the vampires away too (which was funny the first time he said it, but not by the twentieth – it just got boring and sad by then). Toto doesn't care though, he's so cocky about it. It's really funny to see him so pleased with himself. I had to tell him that my digital camera didn't work - and I was *sooo* right – he *had* stolen it – because when my Mum started saying that he'd have to take it back to the shop and that she was going to Bristol next week and if he gave her the receipt she'd go and complain about it, well, Toto got really shifty. Like when Dad used to keep turning the school calendar back to Ms Courtney not wanting any of us to see or anything – well Toto was like that, just sort of moving from one foot to another like he needed a piss or something. I had to try and keep from laughing though, cos Mum kept telling him to go find the receipt and he *sooo* obviously hadn't got one and I knew it all the time but couldn't say anything.

Anyway, I've just realised that the digital camera wasn't broken at all, it just needed a battery in it and I guess Toto forgot to steal that. I ain't going to tell him yet though, cos he's been ragging me about his balls again and that Becky Allen is his girlfriend. He says he did cop a feel and that Kate (her sister) doesn't know nothing and that she's stupid and just wants to be a boy. I don't think she's stupid - she just likes playing with boys cos she doesn't like dolls and make-up and things. Toto says that Becky likes playing with boys too.

Kate is cool cos she's a grunger, you know - a skater chick? And I'm a grunger too, and there aren't many girl grungers at our school, cos most of them are trendies and rude girls, you know? And they're really into designer stuff, but Kate is cool cos she wears cargoes and hoodies and likes cool music like Linkin Park and Nirvana, like me.

Anyway, there was some big TV programme about made-up bands that people have to win competitions to get in. I think they're *sooo* stupid, I mean like the *Popstars* one that did that song I used to like before I got into nu-metal, like Linkin Park and Nirvana, though they were Grunge, but now they're dead I think, except for the one that's in the Foo Fighters who likes to dress up as women in DVDs and stuff. Anyway, I can't remember their name but they were the real ones. All these Rivals and Gareth Gates and people, well they're just pretending to be popstars aren't they?

They are all so foney, I just hate that foney thing.

Dad says that all music these days is derived from African American slave rhythms and gospel blues music. Toto says it all comes from synthesizers. Mum says she liked the Beatles. I don't know what any of them are talking about. I know I do like Linkin Park and want Toto to show me how to burn a CD and get songs from the internet, but he's on his mobile to Becky again who's been grounded cos she tried to eat Toto's face, and her Mum saw my Mum in Tesco's and she told her. It's so embarrassing that my Mum is a grass. Doesn't she know that Toto is family and you can't grass family up, or somebody will wake you up with a gun in your mouth and drive you into a desert and make you dig your own grave in the sand with a shovel then tell you to kneel down in the hole and beat the shit and blood out of you until you're barely breathing and then fill in the hole even though you aren't even totally dead yet and then break your fingers with the spade when you try and save yourself by pushing your hand up out of the sand.

Doesn't she know that she's going to be a non-person?

I told Toto that Mum is the grass when he stopped slobbering over the fone when he was talking stuff to Becky. He said he doesn't care cos Becky can come out tomorrow and they're going to go and see a film or something.

I'm going to Uncle Terry's party now. Byee!!!

Panton

Friday 27th December

Hiya again. I've decided to write this in my new WWE notebook as Toto and Becky are on the computer trying to find some slushy film to go and watch. Toto is being really nasty to me today, and it's only because Mum found out that he was smoking all the time and it's only because Becky's Mum saw him and grassed him up as well – but he thinks I told her and won't believe that Becky's Mum did it even though Becky said that her Mum did it not me. It ain't fair and now he says he won't teach me to use chatrooms and things cos I'm a grass and he hates me.

I think he is sooo foney these days, it's since he met Becky he wants to act like some big man all the time and that I just get in the way. It ain't fair.

Mum and Dad aren't talking to each other either and it's all because at Uncle Terry's party last nite, which I thought was really cool cos Minto'd got an Xbox. He's cool and would talk to me now that we weren't at school and it was ok again to talk to me – and we played that all night. It turns out that Minto *did* pick that cool book for me and I felt *sooo* bad, cos my Mum had got him a really crappy T-Shirt, that Minto wouldn't be seen buried in, but he was nice and didn't mention it, you know?
But Mum and Dad had a big argument cos Minto's Dad gave my Mum a present and my Dad didn't have one to give to Minto's Mum – Auntie Sheila – and Dad got embarrassed, but it was cool. But when they'd all been drinking Dad got really funny cos Mum kept playing with her hair and giggling a lot when she was talking to

Uncle Terry and Dad got the hump and she said he was being childish and that Terry was an attractive man and that my Dad used to be fun but now all he does is try and be cool and that he should act his age cos he ain't a kid and he might as well wear his cap backwards like Hague who was rubbish, but my Dad thought was really good until they replaced him with someone I can't remember.
They've gone now so I can use the computer again and I'm going to play with some chatrooms and stuff

Later

Hi again, I thought I would write some more now that Toto has come home. We've been playing 'peedo' on the chatrooms. This is such a cool game that Toto made up and we've been playing for ages. It's really easy cos all you do is go to one of these chatrooms – they're like places you can go and talk to people all over the world and Europe and stuff and they can't see you and you can't see them but they just want to talk and hang out.

Toto said you've got to be really sort of careful when you play in chatrooms - you need to make sure you're anonymous – which means that people don't know who you really are so they can't come round your house and grass on you or kill you for pretending to be their brother and saying that you always hated them and want to kill them and next time you see them you will kick shit out of them and that you've been kissing their wife and she likes you and doesn't like them anymore and you always hated them and their breath smells of pig shit – which is the worst smell ever. We went by a pig farm when we went on the school trip to the cottage in Wales (by Bristol) and I saw Dad smoking, but I told you this.

So Toto showed me how to be anonymous by using another website called *Anonymizer* or something like that and this sort of pretends that you don't exist and means nobody can find you, which is really cool when you play Toto's game cos you have to go to a chat room and pretend that you're a peedo.

Anyway, I've been thinking about this whole blog thing though now that I 've played on the internet a bit more than I had when I was like eight or nine or something. I think that maybe I will put it online after all, cos it seems really cool. Toto said he would help me do a website on like *Geocities* or something cos it's free and you can just pick a chat room or some games or something and just add them to your page without having to know what you're doing. That sounds *sooo* cool to me and then I can get people to advertise and make some real money.

I wanted to get a paper round last week cos Matthews has one and you can have one if your Mum or Dad sign a bit of paper and then just give it to the man at the paper shop. Matthews was telling everyone that he gets £9 a week just for posting papers through doors and that means he can get a PS2 game every month even if it's not Christmas or his Birthday or anything. Toto says he's a faggit – but Matthews told me it's cos he's got big bones and not cos he eats a lot. Mum wouldn't sign the bit of paper though so I've got to do the blog after all cos Matthews really boasts and he's my main enemy now, not Minto.

Panton

Saturday 28th December

Man I've had like the worst night ever - worse than detention or school or getting kicked off the computer by Toto and Becky or my Dad finding out that I scratched his car with my bike. Worse than Mum finding out that I tried a cigarette I found in Toto's room with Peter Thomas at the skate park and was sick. Worse than any of them. Worse than having to play netball cos you forgot your kit for gym class. Worse.

Shit. I hate Matthews - hate him hate him hate him. He is *sooo* my enemy now, I hate the fat prick more than Toto when he's being really nasty to me again.

It's Dad's fault. Dad made me go to Matthews' house so that he could see Mr Matthews who always smells of fences cos he paints fences - that's his work and never washes when he comes home.

My Dad wants Mr Matthews to paint our fence. I thought it was really funny when Toto told me, cos that means Matthews' Dad works for my Dad - it's not even a proper job or anything. Matthews' Dad is so lame all he can do is stand in people's gardens and paint their stupid fences and Matthews is the scratter of the school.

I was going to tell everybody that Matthews was the school scratter and everything and I thought it would be *sooo* cool, but then it wasn't cos Mr Matthews told my Dad that Matthews doesn't have many friends come to his house (like it's cos he has no friends – doh!) and would my Dad mind if I came across and played with Matthews while they talk about our fence. And my Dad said fucking Yes!!!

I can't believe that he'd do that to me. Can't he see that Matthews is the fat freak of the school and nobody likes him and now Matthews thinks we're bassoon buddies and that he can come to my house and show me how to build a website cos he thinks he's Mr Website just cos his Dad paid for him to have a domain name and he hasn't got *Geocities* or nothing cos his Dad paid for it. That is *sooo* foney and then we had to go to Matthews' house and it smelled so bad when we got there and all the time I'm saying to my Dad that I would paint the fence or do anything if only we didn't have to go to the smelly scratter Matthews' house. And when we got there it was worse, cos Minto and some of his mates were hanging around and saw us go into the scratter house and saw my Dad talk to Mr Matthews like he was his best friend in the whole world and then Minto sort of waved at me as we went in –I was *sooo* fucking red.

And then the smell hit me and it smelt of wet fur and piss that had got hot. Like the boys' toilets at school in winter when they put the radiators on and everybody pisses up the radiator cos they're so hot the piss just turns to steam and the smell was like that and my eyes were watering and I saw Matthews and I just wanted to cry and he was holding Kate's hand like they were boyfriend and girlfriend and I didn't even know they spoke to each other or anything and I had to try and pretend to smile cos my Dad was watching and threatened to ground me if I did anything nasty to Matthews or mentioned the smell of piss.

And then it got worse and worse *cos Kate is Matthews' girlfriend* and they kept giggling and holding hands and I saw them both go into the Kitchen at the same time to get a Coke and I could see that fat smelly scratter fuck Matthews kissing Kate with tongues and she was smiling and kissing him back with tongues and I couldn't see if she let him cop a feel cos the serving hatch was too small, but he looked so smug when they came back with the cokes and then Matthews said that him and Kate were going for a walk to hang out and that we'd have to play together some other time. Like he was doing me this big favour in playing with me and that it wasn't the other way round and Kate sort of smiled at me like I was the scratty loser not Matthews.

Then I had to stay and listen to my Dad and Mr Matthews talk about fences and sit in the smell of the dog Matthews got for Christmas, even though Kate and the shit faced prick Matthews had taken the dog for a walk. The smell hung in the air and smelt worse than all the shit and piss in the world piled on top and burnt and left to rot.

And the dog is so lame – it's so small and just smells even after it's gone and Kate was fussing it and telling it that it was a really good boy cos it didn't bite Matthews when he put the fucking lead on. As if dogs don't like going for walks and always bite you when you try to take them for walks and really hate it when you feed them or scratch behind their ears and stuff – cos dogs do that don't they?

You're such a stupid bitch Kate and I really liked you but you went out with Matthews and held hands and Minto saw you laughing and saw me crying through the car window when we finally left and now he thinks I'm a kid too and that Matthews is, like, the man.

Matthews is *sooo* my Number One enemy now. *He's gonna get it, Tony, he's gonna get it – pop!*

Panton

Later

I've been looking in *GQ* or it might have been in *FHM* or *Loaded* or something (Danny Smith at school got me a copy of *Loaded* from his brother cos I sort of told him I was writing about magazines and stuff and gave him a programme from Bristol City when they lost to Brentford last year and my Dad took me to the game even though City have a bigger ground than Rovers but we prefer Rovers 'cos they have really nice pasties even if they play in a Rugby ground and all).

Well, like I said, I saw an advert in whatever magazine it was for www.spytech-uk.com and they're advertising all these really cool spy gadgets like James Bond uses and stuff. They've got this pretend gun that's used in the new James Bond movie that Dad got on a fake DVD from his mate at work and all and the gun is a Walther PPK 15 shot C02 air pistol and it's got realistic blowback – so the advert says – and it's made of metal and not plastic or anything. It costs £78.95, but I don't know if that includes delivery and post and packaging or anything cos Toto's on the net at the moment looking for fluffy dogs or something to give to Becky Allen so she'll snog him when they go to the school disco which is on Valentines day which isn't until February which is ages away but he's really into being her boyfriend cos he can cop a feel when he likes and she'is nearly convinced but he wants to get her a pretend dog – cos that will make her wear Kylie shorts and put her arse in his face and stuff won't it?

The other thing I've been investigating is phoney ID cards – so you can go to pubs or buy scratch cards and stuff and have a card that says that you're a plumber or over 18 or something – I don't think I could pretend to be 18 or anything, I haven't even got fluffy balls like Toto and my voice is still really high, but if I can make them then Toto said he'll sell them at school for me and we could share the money cos we'll all be happy then – and you can buy a kit to make them for £10 though they don't kind of stick them in plastic and you have to use Letraset to put peoples names on and stuff. Toto says that Minto would really like one, but I'd probably just give him one for nothing cos I want him to be my friend and he's really cool since we played X-box together and he never made fun of me crying when he saw me and stuff.

Panton

Sunday 29th December

Had a good day today cos Toto finally got round to showing me how to do my own website on *Geocities* and it's so cool the way it's all free and you can just add things like chat rooms and Flash games and I got a really cool fighting game for free from FlashKit.com and it"s on my homepage now and so far I've had like 42 hits, though Toto says that it isn't a real number cos every time I go there it adds one to the count and I've been playing the games all day with Toto and it was probably just us going there, but I don't care. That fat blubber fuck shit Matthews has only got 127 on his count and people at school all looked at that to see his foney phuck pictures with his bitch minger Mum scrubbed out.

I really like my site though. I put a mouse trailer on it and it's got these bits that sort of roll around the screen and say my name in those lights they put outside nightclubs like we saw when we went to see Dad's sister in Spain. She was nice, but didn't speak English too good, and we had this weird yellow wine and lots of rice and fish and stuff and Mum was sick cos she's allergic or something. But my site's really cool, and Toto is gonna find out how to add my blog to it so I can put adverts up and charge people to see it and stuff. Toto made me crack up though when we were doing the settings, cos he put my job as managing director of *Sony,* and when it asked my pet name (like if you've got a dog or something) for the secret security question, he put 'Toto' which was really cool of him and he said I was 32 or something cos kids can't really have *Geocities* sites or something so you have to pretend you're someone else and stuff. Like when we play peedo and pretend that we're cool kids but with puppies and jelly babies that you can only see if you meet us in the woods behind the school and you have to turn up on your own wearing your school uniform so that we'll know who you are and stuff. I just want to find Matthews in a chat room and make him look *sooo* stupid and make him turn up with his lame dog and lame girlfriend in the pissing down rain and stand in the cold and wet while me and Toto have a really cool time playing on *Geocities* or something.

I got another email on my *hotmail* today too. This one is gonna make Dad really rich cos there's this man in South Africa who's got loads of money that was left over from something but he needs help to rescue it from the government. If we help him he'll share the money with us and we're both gonna be really rich and stuff. I thought at first it were some sort of con or something, but all they want is a telephone number to ring you on, and so I sent Mr Parkinsen Theod my Dad's cos I've only got my mobile and he needed home and office ones. Here's Mr Parkinson Theod's email in case you want to help him too.

Attention:
I presume this email will not be a surprise to you. Am an engineer with the ministry of mineral resources and energy in South Africa and also a member of the contract awarding committee of this ministry under the south Africa government
Many year ago, the south Africa government asked this committee to awards contracts to foregn firms, in which myself and two of my partner are leader of the committee, with our good position in this committee, we over involved this contract to the tune of of us$21,500,000:00, to be benefited by me and two other of my partner that are in charge of this contract awarding committee in this ministry.
Now, that the contracts value has been paid off to the actual contractor that executed this job, All we want is a trusted foreign partner like you that we shall front to claim this over involved sum Upon our agreement to carry on this business transaction with you,
the said fund will be share as follow, 75% will be for myself and two others of my partner, 20% will be for you for using your bank account,
5% will be set aside for any expenses that might be incurred by us and you in the process of the document and other formalities that will justify you as the rightful owner of this said fund. You should bear in mind that you will be required to put head together with us, and give this business transaction moral and financially support it required to be successful.
If you are interested and financially capable in handly this business transaction, Kindly reply us through this email address for more details and to let you know what is required of this business transaction to be successful.
Also we request your private and office phone number to open communication with you
Your faithfully,
Parkinsen Theod

Later

I am *sooo* pissed off now, cos for ages and ages I've wanted a digital camera so that I can take as many pictures as I want and sort of play with on the computer with Photoshop or Coral or something and for Christmas Toto got me one and I was like 'cool!' even though he didn't get batteries and stole it from the Gadget Shop and stuff and we haven't got a cable to put the pictures onto the computer and stuff. But I was so happy I'd got the camera and it was really cool and small and went on my key ring and stuff – the one with the chain on so it looks really wicked when I've got my hoodie on and my combats and that. Well, I was really happy, even though you can't really see through the hole so you don't know if the picture is really what you want or anything until you look at it after – but it's ok you know. But I've just been reading Toto's *FHM* and it's got this little bit about the Moni-me digital camera which is about the same size as the one I got but that you can get it from Amazon for £49.99 and it's got a proper little screen on the back instead of the silly hole and when I looked on Amazon it looks really cool and makes mine look really lame and comes with all the cables and a book to tell you how to use it and if it don't work or if you don't like it when you get it, even though it looks *sooo* cool in the picture and all, that you can send it back and get your money back which I would like to do with mine so that I could spend the money on the Moni-me camera except that Toto stole it and hasn't even got a receipt so I've got this crappy shitty camera and it's all his fault and I hate him cos he could've got me this one instead of spending all his pocket money on cigarettes and even the money he stole from Mum's purse which he spent on Becky and her lame necklace, when he could have stolen one of those so easy when we were in House of Fraser in Bristol cos they were on the counter when Mum was trying to find something to make her neck look nice instead of old and like a turkey's for Uncle Terry's party and we were hanging around really bored and Toto kept pointing at the women's underwear and saying that I should buy Kate some cos at least then she'd look like a girl but that was before she became that fat greasy scratter's girlfriend and I cut her off cos she's obviously scum if she likes him and not me.

Dad let us watch *The Godfather* today. That was *sooo* cool – I think it was better than *The Choirboys* but not as good as *Goodfellas* which we watched at Jackie Peterson's house last Halloween. It was really long though and there was loads of sort of talking and stuff but Dad said it was made a long time ago now and that all the other mafia movies were only copying it and foney cos *The Godfather* was made by people who were really in the Mafia and were really made men so that if you insulted one or didn't do what they wanted you to, even if it were really stupid, well all the Mafia people in the world would have to come and kill you with a smile on their face even if they were your brother or Dad or something – they just don't have any choice.

When I'm older I'm gonna be a made man and then I'm gonna find that schmuck Matthews and blow his freakin head off, cos he's like *sooo* shit and smelly and scratty and his dog should be buried under a motorway or taken into the desert and cut up into loads of little pieces. Toto thinks I should beat Matthews up and go out with Kate cos Becky doesn't like Matthews cos he smells of piss. Toto makes me laugh when he talks like that and I don't think Becky really said that I just think he says things sometimes just to make me laugh – but that's cool. He doesn't have to.

We've got a plan though cos Matthews is now Toto's enemy too cos he's my brother and we got blood.

Toto is gonna show me more stuff on the computer tomorrow which is part of the plan to piss off scratty Matthews.

Panton

Later Still

Oh man, just had the weirdest thing, I caught my Dad with his own copy of *GQ* cos first of all I thought it was the one I *borrowed* off Toto and that my Dad had come across it when he was shaking down my bedroom and got to my sock drawer. The music got all slow and heavy like that Wagner bloke from Germany that they make us listen to in Music at school and all, like they play when the bad Nazi guy played by Michael York or someone is searching for the escaped prisoners or Jewish people like Anne Frank and they're hiding in the loft and the mother is holding the baby and has to smother it with a tea towel to stop it crying and giving away their hidey-hole to the bad guy who finds them in the end anyway, cos even though the mother had to kill her baby one of the others knocks over a lamp or a book or something and gives them away and then it's only the young girl who might have been Anne Frank or someone else, I can't remember who, but she escapes and stuff and meets up with gypsies in the mountains – but maybe that was Heidi or something. Anyway, I thought it must have been that *GQ*, but I guessed it wasn't when I saw that the pages opened really easy and it didn't look like it had been dried out or anything.

But anyway, I just went into the garage to try and find my football boots cos I like got asked to play for a footie team who are cool, but some of my friends from school like Pete and Jack and Tommy and that all play for it, and this year they're like loads better than they used to be and have won some games and all. Well Pete's Dad runs the team and like Pete and Jack were giving me grief cos they want a sort of Steven Gerrard ball winner in the middle of the park who can spray the ball about and cover every inch of the park and every blade of grass and I'm the only one they know who can kick the ball over the half way line from a goal kick and don't mind kicking people and all so they asked me to play for them and go to their practice, but you've got to wear proper boots and shinnies and stuff and the last time I saw them they were in the garage so I went there and found my Dad with his trousers down reading *GQ*.

Now I know that sounds weird, but my Dad often takes his trousers off in the garage cos there are loads of weird old chemicals from the man who used to live in our house before he died of his heart breaking cos his wife died and his kids had run away from home years ago cos he was boring or nasty to them or something. Well anyway, he left loads of really old chemicals and Dad doesn't want to get them on his clothes so he takes his trousers off. Like Mum is always telling him to wear old clothes, but he goes to the garage whenever Mum is out or something so he probably doesn't have time to change or nothing.

Anyway, what was really freaky was that my Dad looked embarrassed and put his jeans on and just walked out of the garage and went back to the house, leaving me in the garage on my own with all the poisons and stuff, which he normally just doesn't do ever! Anyway, I thought I'd have a look at his copy of *GQ* and it fell open at the back which is where they have the cool adverts and stuff and the bit where Toto sort of rings in biro all the bits that mention Skunk and Hydroponics and www.blunt.co.uk and all – which I think are kind of druggie things and which Toto pretends he knows lots about but is just being really foney again. Anyway, I noticed that one of the adverts was ringed in biro, but it wasn't like the ones Toto does for magic mushrooms or anything, but it was for these special Blue V pills which cost like £29.99 inc. P&P for eight – which is really expensive each.

Now at first I thought that Toto had rung it with a biro, but thinking about it, this didn't make sense. Anyway, I asked Toto later what these V pills were for and he said that they were a pretend version of Viagra which old people and saddos and that use cos they can't get their dicks hard. He said it was kind of like the stallion cream from Anne Summers parties Mum used to do where they had all those vibrating dicks called dildos that were like really stupidly big and moved around on their own and stuff.

Anyway, I think maybe my Dad was going to buy them or something, but when I asked Mum she just went a bit pale and told me I've got the wrong idea and that they were probably vitamins or something – and looking at the advert it doesn't actually mention Viagra or stuff, so I don't know.

Anyway, I got this email today so I'm gonna forward it to Dad.

Panton

-----Original Message-----
From: Pill Medics [mailto:deals@pillmedics.com]
Sent: 06 January 2003 06:34
To: Pantondivilla@hotmail.com
Subject: Increase your penis size in weeks!

VP-RX Penis Enlargement Pills

Finally!! A medical breakthrough in science has enabled a team of doctors and sex experts to create a pill that is designed to enlarge the male penis by length and width. Our tests show that out of 1,500 test subjects, the average gain after 4 months on DP-RX was 2.94 Inches! Amazing, Permanent results that will last

-Gain Up To 3+ Full Inches In Length
-Expand Your Penis Up To 20% Thicker
-Stop Premature Ejaculation!
-Produce Stronger, Rock Hard Erections
-100% Safe To Take, With NO Side Effects
-Fast Priority Fed-Ex Shipping WorldWide
-Doctor Approved And Recommended
-No Pumps! No Surgery! No Exercises!
-100% Money Back Guarantee
-FREE Bottle Of VP-RX Worth Over $50
-FREE Male Help E-Book Worth Over $50

Click Here

Monday 30th December

Oh man we've done it now. Man oh man oh man. God, we've really done it, really, really gone for it in *sooo* big a way – shit. Can't believe it, I really can't believe that we pulled it off. Man this is *sooo* very cool. So cool so cool so *coool*!!!!

See it all started this morning when scratty Mr Matty turned up to do our fence. Me and Toto we were playing football in the garden – Toto always wants to be Beckham – and he's got like the coolest free-kick and clothes and stuff – but I always want to be like Steven Gerrard cos he's *sooo* much a better player even if he is really weird looking. He stamps on people and stuff if he gets sent off whereas Beckham always gets sent off for really foney stuff like just sticking his leg out and not even kicking people hard or anything. So we're playing Beckham v Gerrard one-on-one, and I'm really murdering Toto 17-3 cos he's not really very good at football or anything even though he thinks he's king kiddie and should be a professional even though he's only 14 and Wayne Rooney had been playing 10 years by then and he's good even if he plays for Everton and they're

Liverpool's (who Steven Gerrard plays for) biggest enemies cos they both live near the same park and probably have fights all the time and stuff.

Well, Mr Scratty turned up and started painting the fence and stuff this really bad green colour that Mum had picked, that looks like camouflage when Mr Tatty puts it on cos it's all in funny patches, and Dad isn't really happy about it or anything and wishes that he'd got somebody else to do it even if they cost more than Scrattyman. Cos Dad pretended to be his big buddy he can't tell him to go away now and has to keep giving him little bottles of Stella which he bought in France when he went to buy thousands of cigarettes cheap that Dad says he doesn't smoke anymore even though he won't give them to Uncle Terry to sell like Mum says he should, and Tattyman drinks them even though it's really cold and damp and a really dumb kind of time to paint anything- even I know that.

Anyway, me and Toto are pretending to still be playing one-on-one but really we're watching Mr Matthews in case we can find out something that would let us get our revenge served cold against his smelly shitty son. Well Mr Smelly starts boasting about how their dog is this great guard dog and how it will stop people trying to get into their house and try and like rob stuff. Toto kept laughing at this and saying quietly to me that a burglar would have to be mad to try and rob the Scratty house 'cos all they've got to steal are fuckin fleas and shit. I was trying not to laugh, but Mr Matthews kept on about this dog been really fierce and better than a Doberman or Pit Bull or something, cos people don't think that they should be scared of it, but that it's really fierce if it doesn't know you.

Anyway, he kept on and on and then suddenly I had an idea and Toto had the same idea at the same time and we just looked at each other and went 'Yeah!' – cos we knew how to get back at the smelly fucker Matthews family.

Anyway, Toto started being really sneaky and asking Mr Matthews about the shit stinking dog and where they kept it when everyone was out and stuff – and Scrattymatty never thought anything of it and didn't have a clue or nothing.

Anyway, we told Dad that we were going the park cos the smell in the garden was really bad – and he looked at Toto to see if he was taking the piss out of Mr Smelly and that, but Toto just looked sort of angelic and said that the paint smell was making me cough and he thought it would be a healthier option for us to continue our game in the unsullied air of our local recreational facilities. My Dad thought he was just trying to be clever again, but he let us go cos he probably wants to go to the shed where he keeps the school calendar again. Anyway, he didn't stop us and he didn't notice that we left the football in the bushes by the front gate and he just went and got Mr Whiffy another *Stella* and talked to him cos you could see he felt like he should.

Later on we went to our tree house – I told you about it – the one we never got round to putting in a tree and it's sort of fallen to bits, but it's got this trap door that when you open it all you see is dead grass, cos we never dug a hole or nothing? Well, we started digging the hole and cos the ground's really light and Toto stole a spade we sort of got it to about 25 centimetres deep, which wasn't enough to put the dog in even with it being in a Head bag we found on the side of the railway and all – but we piled loads of boxes and stuff on top of it and covered it with branches and grass so that it didn't look new or anything. See, our idea had been to get Matthews' smelly dog and tie it up and then make out that their great guard dog had been stolen. Toto wanted to steal the clanger off their burglar alarm as well, but it's on the front of the house and people would've seen him and stuff, so we just took the dog, which was really easy cos it was as stupid as the rest of the family and just followed us when Toto whistled - doh!

The only problem was that the dog got killed when we threw it on the railway line and the train hit it.

Panton

Later

I *sooo* want a Slam Man it looks *sooo* cool. In Toto's magazine it says they're the size of a person except they've got no arms and instead of legs they're like weebles and won't fall down. You can program its computer with different boxing moves and then red lights flash up where you should hit it. There are five red lights on the tummy and three on the face and it looks *sooo* cool cos it's all blue and black apart from the lights and you can really hit it as hard as you want and pretend it'is your worst enemy and they can't do nothing to stop you just hitting and hitting and kicking and hitting them over and over and you could get a baseball bat and crack them over the head and it could be that fat fuck Matthews. I hate him. I could creep up and hit him over the head with a shovel or a lead pipe in the conservatory and it wouldn't matter, nobody would ever know or tell me off cos it's not real but it would still feel *sooo* good and get me fit like a kick boxer by practising hitting and pretending it is that fat slobby smelly scratter and it'll probably help me win fights at school and stuff. It doesn't say, but it looks like it would.

Man if I had like £300 or if Toto could get one in his jacket when we go to Bristol that would be *sooo* cool. But I don't know how big a box a Slam Man comes in. It would be worth getting because it says it will give you 'an aerobic/muscle-toning workout at the same time' which I guess is good. I could put my cap on it too if I had it in the corner of my bedroom, cos I can never find it and stuff.

Panton

Tuesday 31st December

I'm doing this bit in my WWE pad cos it's top secret. See, me and Toto had a big secret pow-wow about what to do about the smelly's dead dog and whether we should grass ourselves up or just ignore it, like in Goodfellas when Joe Pesci kills somebody for looking at him funny and then goes and kills their wife and children and friends and mother and father and all their cousins and friends and all their families just to make sure that they don't come and get their revenge, warm or cold. The way I figure it is this – if we said that it just followed us when we were crossing the railway and then we'd panicked and buried it under our tree house, we could probably blag our way out of it even if people thought we were really trying to hurt the dog, which we weren't. It was just an accident, and as long as Mr Smelly doesn't think about Toto's questions and stuff and put two and two together (like he could - thick shit bastard wanker) and get anything at all - then we should be OK.

But Toto thinks we should go the extra step and really rub it in with Matthews cos he's our enemy and he stole my girl and he's got to be made to pay until there's nobody left standing.

Toto reckons we should be really clever and go in for psychological warfare and see if we can punish their whole family and make them come to bits at the seams and hate each other and want to die. Which sounds cool and he says that he's got a plan so I think we'll try it his way.

Toto's plan is really nasty and really simple and really, really cool. I'm so glad that he's like on my side and my friend again, even if it's only cos Becky gets on his case about Kate coming home smelling of dogs and shit.

What he thinks we should do then, is pretend that we've kidnapped the dog and that nothing has happened to it and send them a ransom note and a lock of its fur so that they know that we mean business cos we're the mob. At first he wanted to cut the dog's head off and leave it in Matthews' bed, but I didn't want to cut a dead dog's head off even if it is a mafia initiation and I don't think Toto really did either. We didn't have a big enough knife anyway.

Anyway, we've went on the computer again and Toto showed me how to make a ransom note so that nobody can know who wrote it.

Hey Scuzbuckit
We got ya dog
If you dont go to
school on first day
back in a dress we
will send ya its head
so Dont call the pigz
or it getz it

Wednesday 1st January

New Year, same old shit.

OK, I keep having these really weird dreams. I don't even know why I'm writing this cos I ain't going to show it no-one, yeah right? Not even Minto - and he's my best friend now. Toto is still my brother but Minto is so cool and he just doesn't take the piss out of me, you know? But anyway, I keep having these dreams and it's like me and Kate and she's tied up on this sort of table like they had in that *Mad O'Rourke's Cow Pie Shop* pub in Birmingham when we went there - the one Dad thought was wicked cos it had these really foney plastic bits of meat hanging from the ceiling and you could have a Desperate Dan Cow Pie which was cool cos it was like a whole meal in this really massive bowl with pastry on top and two horns sticking thru it. Dad said that when he was my age (like ever) there was a comic with this bloke in it who ate whole cows in a pie and the pie was so big that the horns stuck thru and that's what this place was all about. He really thinks we don't know who Desperate Dan is and that they don't have *The Dandy* anymore - doh!

Anyway, the tables they have in there are meant to be like the ones butchers use and stuff and have this fake blood all over them and things. and in my dream Kate was tied to one of them and it was all dark like in *Silence of the Lambs* when Jodie Foster is going up the stairs and the freaky guy who hides his dick between his legs and pretends that he's a girl, well he's hiding out and there's this other girl in like a big pit (Dad said it was a geek pit, cos people used to put geeks in pits and throw chicken heads at them before they had computers and got rich and cool and stuff) - but anyway, Kate is tied to this table and I feel strange cos she's all hot and sort of sweating and smelling funny and I sort of feel really weird and wake-up and I've wet myself. It ain't nice you know? I mean I'm loads too old to wet myself and I haven't done that since I was like seven or something, but at least it wasn't as much as then, I mean I can remember what it feels like, all sort of warm and nice and you just don't want to open your eyes and things and then all of a sudden it goes all cold and horrible and then starts burning your legs - well this was different and all I could see was Kate and I missed her even if she is with that shit schmuck bastard and hates me and thinks that I'm a child, but I'll show her - oh yeah, cos I'm going to be a made man one day and all she'll have is Shittyboy.

Panton

Later

Wow, I found this mad website today. Toto was showing how to download stuff from *Kazaa Lite* - it's kind of a place where you can go and get MP3s like Linkin Park and stuff. I typed in 'Linkin' and pressed OK and there were thousands. I could find their new album and stuff and it isn't even in HMV or WH Smiths or anything yet, but it's in the shops in America and people have made it into MP3s and this *Kazaa* sort of lets you look at what music they've got on their computer and you can pick what you want and they'll give it you for nothing. Toto says they can look at what we've got too, but I put all mine on a CD-R so they can't see nuffin, cos I might get in trouble or something.

Anyway, Toto had gone to put gel on his hair and stuff -, cos he's a tart like Dad says when he's laughing and not arguing with Mum about Terry or anything - cos downloading MP3s take a while and Toto gets bored and stuff. So I was playing with Google and kind of searching for more stuff about Quiksilver cos Dad said he would buy me a Quiksilver T-shirt to put under the Ben Sherman shirt Uncle Terry got me from his mate who's on the market in Bristol and stuff.

Actually, the market's real cool - I went with Uncle Terry (who isn't my uncle - but I told you that) and Minto who's still my friend even though he saw me cry and stuff. Well, we went to this market and it's in this sort of car park which turns into a market at weekends when the people who normally leave their cars there when they go to work aren't going to work I guess. Well, we went there and you could get like rip-off DVD movies really cheap and hoodies for all the real cool bands and sort of fake clothes like Ben Sherman shirts and JCB boots and things that look so much like the real ones you see in Cribbs that you can't tell the difference but are loads cheaper and stuff. It's well cool. Anyway, when we got back Dad got really narky cos Terry'd got me a shirt and stuff and he said he wanted his son to 'wear real clothes not ones thrown together in sweatshops in Leicester by illegal immigrants.' Mum said he was just being stupid cos even the ones you buy in the shops are made in Leicester or Taiwan or Delhi or somewhere and all clothes are made in sweatshops. I asked Minto what a sweatshop was and he said it's like a really cool place rich people go to *not* do exercise and look like tarts. I don't think he's talking about the same thing as my Mum, but he's cool and probably right even if he's talking about something else.

Anyway, I was looking for Quiksilver clothes so that I can print off a picture and show it to my Dad and then I found this really cool site, that had these pictures of people on snowboards and stuff and then real weird words and things. Anyway, there wasn't anyone on their chat room but it said to come back later, so I probably will. The words were weird though - when Toto got back I asked him to show me how to copy them in Word - I always get CTRL-C mixed up with CTRL-X - and that's cool in Word but doesn't work on Internet Explorer and stuff. Anyway, this is what I copied off the site - Toto said if I'd put my Blog on a website I could just put a link in - but he's like really narked cos I've written about him so much - which he likes cos it makes him feel all special - but not happy cos it's just on our computer and not on *Geocities* - so he can't show it to Kate and be the man again. Anyway, this is what it said:

'I AM THE SOUND I AM THE SIGHT I AM THE VOICE I AM THE WORDS THE FEARS THE LOOK AND THE VISION I AM WHAT I AM - I AM THE MOOZE THAT MAKES THE WORLD SING, I WANT TO TEACH THE WORLD TO SING IN PERFECT HARMONY FOR I AM THE WORD AND I

I AM THE WORLD I AM THE PEOPLE FOR I AM THE MOOZE AND YOU CAN NEVER RECOGNISE OR RECONCILE JUST WHAT I MEAN TO YOU FOR I AM THE MOOZE UPON WHICH ALL WILL TELL AND ALL SHALL SPEAK FOR I AM MY MOOZE, YOUR MOOZE AND EACH AND EVERYDAY WE PLAY DOCTORS AND WE PLAY NURSES IN DENS AND BIKE SHEDS AND HOLLOW EMPTY PLACES WITH LEAF SHADOWED SKIES AND FADING SUNS - FOR WE EXPLORE AND WE DEPLORE AND WE WANT MORE OH WE WANT MORE SO MUCH MORE FOR I AM THE DOCTOR AND I AM THE MOOZE AND WE ARE JUST SPACE CADETS FLYING TO OZ OR PLANET X TIDYING OUR BEDROOMS AS WE FLOW AS WE FLY FOR I AM THE DOCTOR AND YOU ARE MY MOOZE AND I AM THE DOCTOR AND I AM THE NEWS AND THE MOOZE FOR GENERATIONS TO COME PIN-UPS TO PLAY, FOR I AM THE DOCTOR OF MOOZE AND I AM THE WORDS FALLING FROM THE HONEYED DEVIL'S LIPS FOR I AM THE AFTERLIFE AFTER-BIRTH AND CONDESCENSION FOR I AM YOUR MIND AND I AM YOUR SOUL AND I AM THE BEGINNING MIDDLE AND END FOR WE ARE ONE AND YOU ARE ME AND I AM THE DOCTOR OF THE MOOZE FOR I AM THE DOCTOR OF YOUR MOOZE AND I AM DOCTOR MOOZE AND MINE WILL IS YOUR WILL AND THINE TIME IS MINE TIME AND I AM FOREVER PLAYING AND WE ARE FOREVER TIED FOR I AM YOUR DOCTOR MOOZE AND WE SHALL PLAY UNTIL TIME STANDS STILL AND WE PLAY THRU TIDES OF DILAPIDATED BUILDINGS AND WE TAKE DRUGS AND FLY TO THE MOON AND WE DRINK GREEN UNTIL WILL

FEEL BLUE AND RAINBOWS POUR FROM A DEAD DOG'S EYE AND DYLAN HAS CHILDREN WITH A BIKE UP HIS NOSE AND LEMON TREES BECOME WRITERS AND FLOWERS BECOME TIGHTER AND CHILDREN FOREVER PLAY FOR I AM YOUR MOOZE AND YOU SHALL NEVER PLAY LIGHT WITHOUT MINE IS THE GUIDANCE AND MINE IS THE MIND FOR CHILDREN PLAY FLETCHING AT TIMES WHEN WE SHALL NOT UNDERSTAND WHY THAT IS - WHY IS THAT - YOU KNOW THE ANSWER MY FRIENDS THOSE DAYS WE THOUGHT WOULD NEVER END FOR I AM THE DANDELION AND I AM THE ROSE AND I AM THE GERBER BUT THOU SHALT NOT TELL, AND THOU SHALT NOT SWELL AND THOU SHALT NOT LOVE DIE DREAM PLAY HOPE DESIRE PRETEND OR DISPLAY FOR MINE IS THE VOICE THE POWER THE GLORY BOX FILLING WITH TIE-DIED DESIRE AND THAT SHALL BE DONE THAT IS MINE WILL FOR I AM THE KINGDOM AND I AM THE GLORY AND THOU SHALT NEVER EVEN IF YOU WANT TO. FOR I AM THE DOCTOR AND I AM THE MOOZE AND MINE WILL SHALL BE DONE'

Cool huh? I mean I don't really understand lots of it but it sounds like it was written by a kid - I mean the site is *wicked* and like the skater pictures are cool and it has Quiksilver adverts and things, so I guess it is all ok. It's just wicked and I think that Doctor Mooze is a really cool name. Doctor Mooze. When me and Toto have a band and are really big and can ring up Mike Shinoda from Linkin Park and ask him if he wants to hang out and maybe play guitars or something.

Well when we *do* have a band I'm not going to be called

Panton anymore, cos that is like *sooo* not a rock star's name. I think I'm going to change my name to Doctor Mooze instead, and then everyone will think I've got a really cool website and I won't even have had to bother doing one myself, you know?

Doctor Mooze

Thursday 2nd January

Oh man, we've got such a cool plan now - I mean we wanted to get back at Mr Fenceman - Mr Whiffycreasote fella - we've been trying to find the right way to do it and now we've got it. I'm like, so made up. It wasn't my idea but I feel like it could have been, cos Tito – which is my new name for my brother cos he keeps telling me what to do and my Dad he says that some guy that used to run Yugoslavia, which is what Serbia and Chechnya used to be called before they split up - well my Dad reckons this Tito bloke used to run Yugoslavia, and he faced down the whole Russian army and it was only when he died that the Berlin wall came down and communism died and Castro lost Cuba to the coffee makers and the Manic Street Preachers and stuff. I don't get this cos they went there and did a concert for Castro and I saw it on *MTV* and they're all fat and stuff now and Toto says they aren't 'relevant' since the guitar player who was really thin and didn't fit in jumped off a bridge or hid himself away and pretended he'd jumped off a bridge and pretended he was dead and stuff - but I don't know.

Where was I? Oh yeah. I mean, my brother, well he came up with this idea where we make Mr Smelly really suffer and I think it is *sooo* cool to make Matthews suffer thru his Dad and if we can get him put in prison so that Matthews hasn't got a Dad anymore and he has to move to a council home for fat scratters in County Durham which is right up north (my Dad says) and he hasn't got any friends cos they've had to move to his Mum's family house cos Daddy is canned at her maj's pleasure - and getting beat up in the showers in Winson Green or somewhere. That's where Fred West hung himself, and it would be so cool if Matthews' smelly Dad hung himself cos then he would be infamous though not famous (Toto says the difference is that

Fred West was funny looking, like the bloke in Supergrass,, but Matthews' Dad looks like the woman in the Bangles that looks like she was in *Sex in the City* but got thrown out cos she looked like a bloke except not that much like a bloke).

Since he started seeing Becky he's talked about TV shows like they're real and I don't know, I think he's gone soft - well I did 'til he came up with this wicked plan. I caught him earlier on in his room and he was watching this TV programme about cheerleaders with pompoms and stuff - you know the ones that look like Britney and stuff before she got into that Justin geezer who used to be in that boyband shit n'sync and stuff after she dumped that weener Prince William , who wants to kill animals and have their blood wiped on his face like he's *Braveheart* and stuff even though he isn't Australian like Mel Gibson or Scottish like Derek McInnes or anything. My Dad reckons Derek McInnes is *sooo* cool, but he plays for West Brom who aren't even as good as Liverpool or Everton, never mind Man United or Arsenal (I think Man United will win the premiership this year even though Arsenal are miles ahead and stuff - I don't know, I just kind of think that Arsenal are too cocky for their own good, but Tito says I don't understand and he's probably right even though he thinks he's better than Rooney, who is so cool - even if he is a bit fat and I think Steven Gerrard is better even if he looks like the bloke from The Coral if you think of him stretched out a bit - when he's in the video for - I can't remember what the song is called but says something like 'and when I'm in that lonely room - ahh-ooohh' - and has a funny, well funnier-looking, bloke dressed up as an American soldier (Tito says he looked like George Patton who I think is the fat old boxer who makes sandwich toasters these days) – Well, him anyway..

Where was I? Oh yeah, Matthews' Dad. We're *sooo* gonna fuck him up - I mean, my bro's plan is *sooo* very cool and I'm *sooo* happy. I'm going to bed now, and I'm *sooo* happy - see you tomorrow.

Doctor Mooze

Later

Oh, I am *sooo* pissed off with Toto - he so takes the piss, I mean I know he's my brother, but I really hate him sometimes. He's so foney and then he's like a total prick. Did I tell you, yeah, that he stole my digital camera so he and Becky could take coo-coo pictures and email them to each other and be really pukey.

Well, I kept the USB cable Mum got me from Argos (I said I'd lost it, didn't grass Toto up or nothing) so he had to ask me to put the pictures on the computer and then he'd have to give me the camera. Well, he was like really angry cos he thinks I want to look at pictures of the top of their heads when they're kissing - cos it's the only picture he can take of them both (yeah right - sure I do) - so he got really narky and kept threatening me and stuff and then Mum told me I had to have a bath. Well, just as I'm getting out Toto comes in and takes pictures of me covered in soap. I'd been dozing and having that dream again and it was so embarrassing cos, like, I think I'd wet when I was in the water. My willy was all funny and Toto took a picture and won't give me the camera until I give him the lead - and I'm really scared that he'll show Becky and she'll tell Kate and she'll tell Matthews and everyone at school will know and I'll have to go away and become a monk in Spain like Sean Connery in that old film where people kept killing monks by making their thumbs go black. I fuckin hate him the bastard bastard bastard.

Doctor Mooze

Later

Toto gave me my camera back and said he hadn't shown the pictures or emailed them or anything to anyone and I deleted them and you couldn't see anything much anyway. I still hate him, but not so much

Night night!

Doctor Mooze

Friday 3rd January

Hiya Well, today was weird and stuff and I never thought I would but it was Toto's idea and I can see what he means and stuff, even though I didn't want to or anything, but even if Matthews was playing the big man with Kate and kept on going to the kitchen with her to cop a sneaky feel and stuff it was still cool cos Minto came and just took the piss out of Matthews all night and kept telling him that he was gonna make him his bitch at school and that he'd give him grief so much that he'd wanna die and stuff. And Minto kept asking him where his shitty little dog had gone and was he guarding the great busy motorway in the sky

I'd told Minto about Matthews' dog even though Toto told me not to cos it was a family secret bound by blood and tradition - but I asked Minto not to tell anyone and he said he wouldn't and I believe him but I did get nervous when he was taking the piss out of Matthews - but I don't think the dumb fattyman would suss it anyway, so I didn't say anything to Minto.

Anyway, I was finding it really hard to be nice to Matthews even though Toto said to go to his party and pretend to be his friend cos you should always keep your friends nearby but you should always keep your enemies closer or something - like they said in Goodfellas or Scarface - which is such a cool film - or maybe the one where that fat guy talks with cotton wool in his mouth, least that's what Toto says but he could be being his foney self, but it sounded like it anyway.

So I went to the party and Minto came and it was pretty cool and Kate's friend Tiffany was being nice to me and kept following me around and Minto said that he thought she had the hots for me and she kept offering me slices of her pizza, which I didn't want but it made me feel good. But tonight wasn't about having a good time cos Toto had given me a job to do and if you don't follow orders you can be thrown out of the family and become a non-person and everyone will turn their backs on you, like when Sol Campbell went back to Spurs for the first time after he moved to Arsenal - and I hate them and think it must be weird cos everyone is French, though I guess it's the same at Liverpool and stuff - though my Dad says they all used to be Scottish when Liverpool were as good as Man United are now and always won stuff - but that was a long time ago and football wasn't even on TV in colour then.

But the party was OK cos Minto was funny and kept telling Kate that she should find herself a real man and saying that Panton was Spanish for Stud whereas Matthews was English for Wanker - and everyone laughed, which was cool. Even Kate smiled and I felt all funny again and forgot about pizza girl and it made me really proud to be following my mission cos I knew that it wasn't just revenge, it was so I could get Kate to come and be my girlfriend and dump Matthews cos that's what I really want even though I'd never tell Minto or Toto or anyone in case they laughed, but I can't stop thinking about her and it's always then when I wake up.

Doctor Mooze

Later

Hi again, I had to get up to write this cos it was the most important bit about going to Matthews' party and I got into stuff about Kate and Minto and that and forgot to write it - doh!

See the thing I had to do was give Matthews a copy of Cubasis VST which me and Toto had downloaded from Kazaa - cos Matthews is too lame to know how to do that even though he thinks he's Mr Internet and has his fancy domain name and all - but that don't matter. You see, Matthews has been telling everyone for ages how he's this super DJ and that and even Kate said he was OK - cos his Dad had got him these really expensive decks and lessons at Christmas last year and Minto had seen them and said they were cool but Matthews played them like a 'white boy Nigga wannabe' which is how he talks and stuff - I mean my Dad would kill me if I said 'Nigga' and Toto too, but it's weird cos when I asked Minto why it was ok for him to say it but not for me, he thought it was funny and then he said:

> 'If you (like he meant me) call me a Nigga you're oppressing me based upon my skin colour and the fact that at one time my ancestors were dragged in chains from their home and families in darkest Africa, packed into airless ships, taken across the ocean and put to work in fields picking cotton as slaves. If however, I call myself a Nigga it's ok because it's in recognition of the truth that despite the fact that at one time my ancestors were dragged in chains from their home and families in darkest Africa, packed into airless ships, taken across the ocean and put to work in fields picking cotton as slaves; despite this and the reality that many thousands died on the ships, were raped by their new owners or generally treated as scum - despite all this, I am now sitting here and talking to you as, at worst, an equal, but more probably as a superior

> and yet even if I were still that slave, even if the world was still a darker place than it is now - even with all such things, I would still be sitting here either as your nigger or with you as mine, but still I'd be sitting here, smug in the knowledge that I am hung like the hottest donkey this side of hot donkey world - and every bitch in the place wants a piece of me'.

I had to write that down a while after, so I might have got bits wrong, but by the end of it all everyone in the place was quiet and stuff, apart from Minto (who had said it all in this voice like Chris Eubank, who used to be a boxer but now, well I don't know what he does) - yeah except for Minto who was laughing. Anyway, but I was talking about DJ chunky and all and how he is Mr Hotdex - Not!

Me and Toto had got Cubasis which is this really cool recording studio software that lets you record your mixes on a computer as though it was a real recording studio and then you can kind of re-mix them and put them on to MP3 and put them on the internet or even burn them on to a CD-R and sell them as white label demos and get a recording deal if they're good. Well I know Matthews has been saving his paper round money to buy Cubasis (cos people really pay for software, don't they, when you can just go on Kazaa and download it for free, and I mean Matthews has got broadband from Telewest or Blue Yonder or whoever they are and we're stuck with this Tesco's 56k modem crap which is the only thing my Dad will pay for). But anyway, Toto had burnt a CD-R with Cubasis on it and all I had to do was install it on Matthews' shitty computer and that would be cool.

Where was I? Oh yeah, so anyway later on at the party, Minto was talking to Kate cos I asked him to and I said to Matthews that I was going to go soon so if he wanted Cubasis we'd better go and put it on his computer and stuff cos I had to give Toto the CD-R back because he didn't want anybody else to have a copy and that especially not Matthews (this wasn't true but it was all part of what Toto called our smokescreen cos he didn't want to leave any evidence that could be traced back to us and all). Anyway, Matthews knows that Toto doesn't like him much and stuff so the story sounded right. But I could see that he was really worried that Minto would steal Kate off him and make her his bitch or something, and was distracted and all. Anyway, I just pretended to get real shitty and said that if he didn't want it I just wish he'd stop pissing me around and treating me like a bitch and all - and he was like 'no, no' and stuff cos he really wants Cubasis and all but really was worried about Kate and Minto and that maybe Minto would steal her from him even though Minto is loads older and cooler and would be embarrassed to be seen with Kate cos she's a kid and everything and a skater-girl whereas Minto says that he isn't Grunge and he isn't Rude – 'I'm an individual' - but Matthews is dumb like that and doesn't really think it through.

Anyway, Matthews *did* really want Cubasis so he said that we should go to his bedroom where he has his computer. Now I've never been in his bedroom before and I guess I didn't really know what it was going to be like - but when we got there it was awesome. I could see he was being really foney cool as we went in cos he knows how awesome it is and everything, and I could see he was just waiting for me to say something, but I wasn't going to make his day by doing that, not if he'd buried me up to my neck and had lobsters crawling toward me. No, not lobsters - those insect things with pointed tails that curl up behind them and sting you and all and live in deserts (though Dad said he used to see them in Birmingham when he lived their years ago, but we don't believe him cos when he talks about Birmingham it's like this mythical place where his football team - West Brom.

- were good and there were curry houses every 20 metres and stuff and they have scorpions). Scorpions - that's it. No, not even if they had scorpions coming towards me would I have ever said that Matthews' bedroom was the coolest place I had ever been anywhere ever, even though it was. See, when I went in it was dark cos he's got these chrome cover spotlights in the corners of the room and this bar going across the ceiling with a few more on - but they were moving - like search lights or stage spotlights or something - and in the corner of the room he'd got this enormous space ship lava lamp which was *sooo* cool I just wanted to hit him there and then, but I had to be professional and everything and remember my mission so I didn't, but I wanted to - but the best thing was the whole of the wall when you walked in was painted like the cover of Linkin Park's album *Hybrid Theory*, which is the best painting in the world and it even had the words so they looked right, not like when people paint Linkin Park on the back of their bags at school and stuff, but this was proper cool. And then I saw the CD player he'd got, which was tiny and shiny with all these cool lights on it. It had speakers all over the room, real little Bose ones like you see in *GQ* and stuff, but no leads anywhere cos they were wireless and then I saw his computer and it was this iMac looking thing which I've seen in PC World at Cribbs that costs thousands and has got a 3Gig chip and a gig of memory and all and must really be cool and quick and you'd be able to play games really fast and stuff. But I could see that Matthews was waiting for me to say something and I was so desperate not to make him feel like 'the man' even though he'd got the coolest room in the whole world and stuff and I was really jealous and really, really wanted it to be my room, and I could see why Kate would want to be with someone who had such a really cool room and that our plan seemed so small now, and that even if it worked and Kate dumped Matthews she still wouldn't want to be with me cos my bedroom is pants compared to the awesome one Matthews has, but even though I was thinking all this only a second had gone past and my brain was zooming along like one of those weird adverts that are all in fast forward - no, it was more like in The Matrix when everything goes in slow motion except you and I could have jumped in the air like a ninja and kicked Scratty-matty a hundred times before his fat flabby brain caught up and knew what had happened and he would've been dead before he hit the dirt and even though he'd got a real cool room it was still quite dirty, it was just that you never noticed at first cos of the cool lights and it still smelt of wet dog and piss even though his dog was dead and buried and getting even smellier under our tree house. And that's when I remembered that our mission was more about putting Scratman DJ in his place cos it isn't about money it's about cojones and mine are the biggest muffas in the whole of this shitty town. I just looked at Matthews and said quietly that his Linkin Park picture was cool - he looked smug and stuff and waited for me to carry on and that was when I pulled him into my little trap, cos I looked him in the eye and kept my expression real cool like Joe Pesci and said :

'Like, what was your favourite song on the album then?'

And you could see he wasn't expecting that and he sort of stuttered a bit and then I knew, that was when I knew for sure that all the cool things he'd got, the cool computer, the wicked stereo the absolutely brilliant Linkin Park picture - all of it was completely fake and had nothing to do with Matthews - I knew he didn't know how to use the computer and I knew that the stereo was only cool cos his Dad had paid loads of money for it, and Kate had said that she thought it was funny that Matthews wanted to be a DJ but didn't have a turntable other then his mixers, and most of all I knew that Matthews hadn't done the painting himself cos I was in his art class last year and he was shit, I mean he was really, really bad, and still Matthews was waiting for me to carry on talking but things had changed in my head and I knew I had all the power again and that I had to complete my mission even if I died in the process and never saw Kate again or anything. Matthews was still waiting, but he'd got a funny look on his face like he wasn't so sure that he was still in control but didn't know why. And then I heard Kate laugh downstairs and Minto talking really loud, and Matthews jumped and I could see that he was scared that Minto was taking his girl (as if - doh!) and before I could say anything, he started for the door and said, 'Would you mind putting Cubasis on the PC and I'll get some drinks' - like he was doing me the favour and like he was reclaiming all his power so that he was the man again and I was just this little kid - but he couldn't put me down this time as I knew - I fuckin' knew now and he could never treat me like shit again - cos I was the man and I had his number and it was 333, the number of the coward, it was number two - the colour of shit. I just looked at him and said

'Linkin Park have got a new album out - are you going to paint that cover on the wall as well?'

And he looked stunned, like one of the rabbits when we line them up at night with the Maglite - right in the eyes. They look like they're scared but don't know why and then you pop them - and Matthews just looked at me and stuttered again, 'I, er, didn't paint it - my Dad got someone to do it' and I just looked at him and even though my brain was shouting and screaming 'foney fuck foney fuck foney fuck' all I did was just shrug a bit and say, 'Oh, I thought Kate said that you'd done it yourself - she must have got the wrong idea, mustn't she?'

And I just left it hanging in the room and sort of walked to the computer - the threat that I would just 'mention' it to Kate hanging around like the smell of Matthews' dead dog - and he just stood there looking at his shitty painting in his shitty room and he just became so small - and then Kate laughed again and he went pale and muttered something and just sort of turned round and left. And there I was, there I was sitting in front of his computer, sitting there with Cubasis on a CD-R and an empty CD drive in front of me and Cubasis on a CD - Cubasis and a few other things that Toto had put there so that we can complete our mission and get revenge.

First things first though, and I got out my WWE notepad and copied down the *hotmail* email addresses and password that was really securely stuck on the side of the computer in case it came in useful and stuff – they're so dumb - it had Matthews', his Mum's and his Dad's email addresses and passwords just sitting there – doh!. Anyway, next I put in the CD-R, and it was all over in a minute or two and I took the CD-R out again and broke it in half. The crack sound was loud but I couldn't hear it properly cos there was this rushing sound like when we used to play in the water pipe by the river and you could hear the water rushing along and it was like it was going to catch you and wash you away into the sea without a lifebelt and stuff and Minto's book doesn't cover that - and I didn't even have the book then but that's how it sounded and I just put the pieces of the CD-R in my pocket and stood up and went downstairs and Minto looked at me and raised his eyebrows, and he was talking to Kate and making her laugh, but he was doing it for me cos he's my best friend and he knew I had to do something and that he had to keep Matthews out of my way in case he realised something wasn't right so he was my diversion and when he raised his eyebrows he was asking me without talking whether it was cool - and I just nodded really slightly so nobody except Minto could see and he just smiled and nodded a little bit himself and then stood up and said really loudly, 'Well that's enough of playing with the kiddies for one night - I'm going out for a bit of grown up fun.' Then he took a step away from Kate and Matthews and looked across at me again as he was putting on his really cool Ben Sherman jacket and said, 'Hey, my man, are you coming with me then, or are you staying with the children?' and it took a second for me to realise he was talking to me and not one of his friends and then I knew and could see him smiling his little smile at me and I just felt *sooo* cool and grown up and in control like when I was in Matthews' room and I just grabbed my Quiksilver hoodie and said real cool- like, 'Yeah, why not' and then we just walked out and I had to try and be really cool and stuff but I could see Kate's face and she looked at me like I was really cool and I saw Matthews' face and he looked like he'd just lost everything and didn't know how or why it could happen to him on his birthday or ever , but he didn't realise that it was only the start - and all I could hear in my head was this Dick Dastardly laugh and I felt so cool and it was the best night of my life or ever as me and my friend Minto walked back to my house and he made sure that I was alright and all the time he kept calling me king-kiddie and laughing at Matthews - even though he only thought I was messing up his computer and didn't know our real plan.

I better go to bed now, cos I've been typing for ages now and it's 4 am and I'll get killed if I get caught

Doctor Mooze

Panton beating Tito at footie

Saturday 4th January

Hiya! Man I've had such a cool day today, I mean yesterday was wicked with Minto and stuff cos he really helped me and made me feel good by showing everyone at the party that I was his friend and that he wasn't bothered that I'm loads younger than him or anything and that even though I am he still wanted to hang out with me and that he thought that Matthews' party was really *plebby* and I could see that Kate was really impressed and that she thought Matthews looked like a real jerk and all when we left. I had that dream again last night but this time I was trying to undo the chains from Kate and she was shouting 'hay-elp' like Penelope Pitstop in the cartoons where she's got that real pink racing car that looks cool and not a Barbie car or anything even if it *is* pink and in my dream I managed to get Kate off the table and she hugged me and kissed me on the cheek and it was *sooo* nice you know? And she smelled so nice, not like piss or anything like Matthews' house, but like a flowery day, like when we go down the beach in the summer in Weston and cut thru Jill Dando's garden which was made by that bloke with the funny eyes and the woman who's always lifting loads of stuff and sort of wobbles cos she ain't got a bra on. That's what my dad says anyway, and he's always watching it. But, I mean,yesterday was cool, but today was better even though it was in a different way.

I didn't go to a party or see Minto or Kate or anything, all I did was sit at the computer with Toto, but it was so cool cos we were putting the plan into action and Toto was explaining it a bit more and stuff and telling me about BackOrifice which is this really cool hacker tool that he downloaded from the Doctor Mooze website or somewhere and it lets you take over other people's computers without them knowing it and lets you see what they're doing on their screens and stuff. It felt *sooo* cool cos we could look at Matthews' computer cos I'd managed to load Cubasis VST onto it and Toto had put some extra bits on the CD and even though I was really impressed with Matthews' bedroom and stuff I arranged for Minto to talk to Kate and didn't let Matthews think he was the man or anything so he left me alone to do it and Toto has been calling me 006½ all day cos he says I was like a real secret agent and that he's proud of me and I don't think he's ever said that he's proud of me before ever, even when I won a swimming race at school or when I got an 'A' for English, even though Dad made a big deal of it and we all went to a Harvester for tea and I had this massive ice-cream with nuts on it and stuff and it was really creamy and Toto was allowed to have a steak to himself and a glass of wine which made him feel so grown up that he even forgot to steal any knives or spoons or anything and he even takes stuff in Wimpy when we go there.

But with this BackOrifice thing it is really cool cos we were able to have a look at all the stuff on Matthews' computer cos he leaves it on the net all the time cos he's got broadband and stuff and it doesn't cost per minute like our crappy 56K cheapo effort does, and we copied all these files of his dad's over to our computer with all the accounts for his business and stuff and then we changed some of the numbers so that he'll charge my dad loads less and then Toto didn't think that was enough so we just made up loads more numbers then put them all back onto Matthews' computer so that you couldn't even tell we'd changed them, but then Matthews must have come in with Kate and stuff cos Internet Explorer opened and I kind of jumped up and tried to switch the computer off in case they could see us and Toto was killing himself laughing cos I thought that we could be seen even though he told me that we couldn't.

But anyway, then we went into spy mode which is really cool and sneaky and we just sat there and watched Matthews and maybe Kate (who I think I love but won't tell Minto or Toto or anyone in case they laugh at me and anyway I want to tell Kate first and she'll hug me and kiss me on the cheek). But we were watching for ages and they went to really crap sites like *Gareth Gates* and *A1* and *Blue* and stuff, but then it got really funny cos they went to this site where you can get loads of things for free just by giving your name and address and stuff and then loads of companies send you stuff thru the post - me and Toto ordered all these free books and sticker albums and stuff from it later on which will be well cool when they arrive cos I want to collect the stickers for all the Premiership footballers and this means I don't have to buy the album or anything, but Matthews and maybe Kate were going to all these sites for face creams and stuff and trying to get free samples - I think they must be for Kate though Toto reckons that boys use them too sometimes and seemed kind of foney and weird when I asked how he knew that and he said that it's because he read about them in *GQ* - but I think they must be for Kate cos there were loads of them and Matthews has got loads of spots and doesn't wash I think, cos he always smells the same - bad, so they must be for her.

And then I got really angry cos the name where they were telling the websites to send the free creams to was *Mrs Kate Matthews* and they were going to Matthews' address and I got really pissy but Toto said that it doesn't mean that they've got married and Kate hasn't moved in with Matthews or anything - it just means that they were using a fake name and age and stuff like when we set-up my site on *Geocities* and that Kate probably wasn't there at all and that Matthews was just embarrassed cos he was getting them for himself or that he was really tight and was trying to get as many free things as he could so that he could give them to Kate for her birthday - and then I realised that I didn't know when Kate's birthday was and got really upset and stuff and angry cos Matthews will know and I don't - so Toto rang Becky to find out and it's May 22nd so they probably aren't for her and Matthews put July 22nd anyway which probably means that he was on his own and that the creams were probably for him anyway.

I called him a foney cheap bastard and Toto laughed and said that there's no pleasing me.

Anyway, after a while it was getting boring cos Matthews had gone to every cream site on the *freeukstuff* website and there were loads there like Clinique, Estée Lauder, Roc, Nivea, Ponds and Clarins and a few others I forgot

Anyway, after a while they must have gone or Matthews had gone to bed or something cos nobody was using the computer so me and Toto we decided to send loads of other things to Matthews' address and get them to send them to Mrs Kate Matthews just in case he'd decided to just give them to Kate for her birthday or for some stupid anniversary or something, so we went to loads of sites like *Durex* for condoms, *KY* for some kind of jelly that Toto thinks is funny. I asked him why and he wouldn't tell me - though I think it was because he doesn't know – he's such a foney and it doesn't really say on the website.

And then we went to this other site called *Goldspot* which sells sprays that make your breath smell good, which Matthews really needs but Toto says isn't something you'd want to give your girlfriend if you want her to kiss you or even talk to you again. And then we ordered loads of air fresheners and stuff to try and help Scrattymatty make his house smell a bit nicer (though they only come in small bottles so I can't see that it'll help) and then we found a site where they sell extra-strong deodorant or anti-perspirant - I don't know what the difference is - called Mitchum which is for people who really sweat loads even when it's not midsummer and stuff and probably wear blue long-sleeve shirts and have dark patches down their backs and under their arms like Lee Evans the weird looking comedian that dad likes but isn't funny.

Anyway, that was really good fun, but it's got a bit boring now so we're going to wait for Mum and Dad to go to bed and then we're going to put the next part of our revengey plan into action which means I've got to find the book Minto gave me cos we need to know how to break into the school though Toto is being all secretive (I think it's cos he didn't get to be 006½ last night and he's jealous) and anyway, he won't tell me what we're going to do.

Doctor Mooze

Sunday 5th January

Oh man, last nite was so cool. See me and Toto we decided to put the next stage of Toto's plan into action - I like that 'put the plan into action' - it sounds so *Choirboys*, sooo very *Goodfellas* . Toto's plan is *sooo* dark *it just like kills me, Louis.*

Anyway, we went for two stages. First of all we decided that we had to keep the pressure on Matthews and all, so we decided that we'd do another ransom note for his shitty-smelling dog - I mean it's dead and all, but he don't know that, so we might as well make the most of it. Anyway, we did another ransom note on the computer so that it couldn't be traced or anything - like before except we made it so that he had to do some real stupid stuff and we made it so that he might be caught doing it and look really shonky and an idiot and stuff. So we decided to tell him to take loads of stupid stuff to Ms Courtney and then he's got to go find his next clue so we can make him trail all over the place and then look like a dumb ass and Kate will think he's really strange and pathetic and dump him and then look across the room at me and feel all warm inside and realise what a fool she's been and come across and say 'Hey Panton' and I'll say 'Hey' and she'll ask me to go to the Mall, like we're American or something and then we'll maybe go to *Pizza Hut* and have all we can eat for five pounds - except I haven't got five pounds, but Toto would lend it me, I reckon, if it meant that he wouldn't get grief about Kate smelling like piss cos she's hanging around with *him*.

Anyway, the ransom note – we snuck up to Matthews' house and put it under the door in an envelope that looked like it was from a girl, you know, I mean we stole some of Mum's scented paper and stuff and wrote it really neat and all - so that he'd grab it and hide it from his folks. Anyway, the note said:

if you want to see your dog
again deliver 14 dunkin donuts,
40 marlboro and an
enormous dog turd to
14 the grange
on Tuesday and leave
it on the doorstep,
knock the door and
run around the corner
where you will
find instructions
where to find your dog

Later

We've been playing spies again, this time it's been a lot better cos Toto suddenly had an idea and asked me whether I'd noticed whether Matthews had a webcam on his computer and I thought there was one on top of the screen so we started BackOrifice again and Toto was kicking himself and everything and calling himself dummy, cos he hadn't thought of it before and when we connected to Matthews' computer this time all he had to do was turn on the web cam and there it was - we could see most of Matthews' bedroom. The picture wasn't great or nothing cos we've got this shitty connection, but Toto set it up so that it just refreshed every second, so it was all jerky and stuff but we could see everything, even his really foney Linkin Park picture and we could see Matthews, and Toto made the window big and even though it was a bit sort of distorted you could see if you sort of squinted your eyes, cos the blockiness blurs and it is a bit clearer. Anyway - it was cool.

Me and Toto just looked at it really quietly, cos it was brilliant and Toto said 'This takes our whole plan and observation on to a different level of sophistication' - I just gave him a look and he laughed and went red and said 'well it does' but I think he realised that I thought he was been foney and got embarrassed about it, which made me laugh but only to myself cos he's being cool and I don't want to piss him off or anything and spoil it. You see, Toto, he always has these real dark moods, you know? He'll be all cool and nice and everything for days and days and then for no good reason he'll get really upset about something – like if the salt is in the wrong place on the table or somebody has opened a window or something. Mum says it's cos he's growing up and is a teenager, but I think it's just cos he's an arsey twat sometimes and just likes to always get his own way and be right and have everyone think he's the man.

Anyway, the reason we wanted to spy on Matthews this time was to see what he would do about the second ransom note we'd left him, cos Toto thought that maybe he might not do like we told him to do and take all that stuff to Ms Courtney's house and find the next note and stuff and that he might go to the police and they'd have all these coppers pretending to be kids at our school and that nobody would notice even though they would all be old enough to smoke and shave and stuff like in Beverly Hills 902510 and Buffy. I thought he was being stupid, but I can see what he means. And anyway, Matthews came across to his computer and it was really weird cos I could see him walk across and sit down in front of us and stuff like we were looking at him down a tunnel or something and then Internet Explorer started and he was picking his nose. Even though I knew he couldn't see us or hear us or anything I still covered my mouth so he couldn't hear me laughing and so did Toto when he grabbed this really big bogey from up his nose and then started rolling it on the desk so it was like a worm, like we used to do with Playdoh or Plasticine when we were loads younger. It was so gross cos he kept sticking it to his forehead and then peeling it off and this bogey must have been enormous cos it looked like a big scar on his face even over the webcam with the window not being that big. Then he totally grossed us out, he put it in his mouth and sucked it in like spaghetti. I just wanted to hurl - he really is the grossest bastard in the whole world and Kate is gonna be *sooo* rid of him and that is when Toto really started wetting himself and told me.

See, I didn't realise everything you can do with webcams and stuff but Toto told me that he's been recording Matthews all the time and it was just sitting on Matthew's computer waiting for us to download later - and that we can put it somewhere so that people from school can see it and then they'll all know. But we'd have to do it secretly and stuff cos we don't want anyone to know that we've used BackOrifice on him or anything.

Anyway, Matthews was obviously not really sure what to do about the ransom note, cos he started looking at these sites that are like *Friends Reunited* but for people who have lost their pets - like *Pets Reunited* if it exists which it probably does in America cos they have all these lame sites for anything you can think of - and that was what it was like for Matthews cos every site he went to was all about Mrs Mulkovic who'd lost her pet dog Splurge in Cincinnati or Mr Yackup who was trying to find Iggy his pet tarantula and stuff - which was all funny but not 'Hey Matthews we found your dog, and it's so clever and smells so nice and it's just waiting for you to take it for a walk' which he must have been hoping for I reckon.

But anyway, me and Toto got real bored with all that, so we went out and played football and stuff for a while until we had to come in and eat tea.

Doctor Mooze

Later

I have just had the funniest time. See when we went out to play footie I totally stuffed Toto 9-3 in one-on-one and I was like Jason Koumas from West Brom who is the coolest player even though West Brom aren't very good and though Toto kept saying he was Rooney he plays like a girlie loony, but anyway after we'd come in and had our baths, Toto called me in to look at the computer cos he'd left BackOrifice on so it recorded what Matthews had been doing and he'd downloaded the Mpeg to our computer sort of automatically using FTP - which is how you can copy things around really easily.

Anyway, we kind of skipped thru the file and it was all Matthews looking at boring websites and stuff which was really yawnsome for ages and ages, but then he gets up and looks really shifty and goes to his bedroom door and looks out, then shuts it and just stands there sort of hopping from one foot to the other like he's trying to work out a really hard maths sum or like he's about to piss himself or something. Anyway, he opens the door and has another look and there's obviously nobody around cos he goes, all sneaky, across to his wardrobe and kneels down in front of it and opens the door. Then he reaches inside and there must have been carpet on the floor inside cos he moved these trainer boxes out and on to the floor then lifts a bit of carpet which must have been cut out – and, not thinking, I said, 'Hey Toto - he's got a secret place cut out of the carpet just like yours' which was really dumb cos Toto wasn't meant to know that I knew he'd got a secret hideaway and he gave me the third degree about how I knew and if I ever looked in there he'd kill me and stuff. I don't know why he was so bothered cos he's only got dumb magazines and condoms in there and it ain't like he's going to use them cos they're nearly past their sell-by date and all covered in dust and stuff. Anyway, I never cracked with Toto and he wanted to watch the Mpeg as well so he let me off light this time, but I know he'll move his magazines and stuff - but that's cool, 'cos I'll find them again.

Anyway, out of his hidey-hole, Matthews started getting these newspapers and stuff and started laying them on the floor, but we couldn't see what they were. I thought they might be football posters, but I don't remember Scrattymatty liking football or anything and Toto thought they were probably popstar pictures, but anyway, as he got more and more out they were getting closer to the computer and the webcam so we could begin to see what they were and they were pictures of topless women - like Page 3 of the *Sun* or something - and I started laughing so much, cos who'd be so lame as to hide away Page 3 pictures which you can see everywhere?

I mean he's got the internet and everything and you only have to type in 'XXX' to find tons of pictures and stuff without trying and lame Matty is cutting out Page 3 pictures then hiding them in secret holes in the carpet.

Man I thought it was so funny, and Toto is laughing too, but telling me to be quiet cos we were meant to be going to bed and stuff. Anyway, then it got even funnier cos Scrattyman went and got a catalogue out of his wardrobe like *Grattans* or *Kays* or something like Mum uses to order clothes and we couldn't see what page he was looking at but I looked at Toto and we both just *knew* that he was looking at the women's underwear section and that he was really getting off on it. Man it was funny, and I was crying and stuff and Toto's saying 'oh wow, look - this woman, I can see this woman... *in her Bra*' - in this really shocked voice as though he was Mattyman and had discovered something really shocking. It was really funny, and we were really laughing and then Matthews started undoing his jeans and we both stopped dead and went really quiet and Matthews started to put his hands in his fly and Toto just sort of went 'oh shit' and stopped the Mpeg and went quiet, and then after a little bit that felt like a really long time cos we were both standing there really shocked, Toto started laughing again and said, all quietly and whispered so that only I could have heard even if anyone else had been there, 'See Panton, I always said he was a wanker', and then he started laughing again and said 'that's perfect, we've really got him now' and then even though he wasn't laughing anymore I could hear this really fake scary horror film laugh like off *Scooby Doo* or something and that was it.

Doctor Mooze

Monday 6th January

Well we did it, we like really did it - we really made that bastard Matthews suffer. We really got him exactly where we want him and *we gonna play him like a kipper, Paulie* - we gonna strip him bare and hang him out to dry – an' ain't that the truth?

See, today is the day we said for Matty to deliver his ransom to Ms Courtney's house so that he might get his shitty-smelling worthless dog back. And…he did it! He really went there with all the crap we told him to take and just walked up her driveway, like it was the most normal thing in the world. He just put the ciggies and donuts and dog turd down right on the porch carpet - he even opened the door of the porch, put everything down and then shut the door behind him, like he was scared someone was going to nick it and then he wouldn't see his li'l poochy dog again. Man, me and Toto, we sort of hid in a bus shelter just up the road, outside the fish shop and we could see him, cos Ms Courtney has got her house in this little grove place, but right on the corner so really it's on the main road as well, but I bet she puts the grove as her address not the main road, cos teachers are like that and always try and foney things up so that they sound better than they are, even, if it doesn't matter or nothing. Anyway, Matty closes the door of the porch and stands there a minute as though he's waiting for his doggie-woggie to run up and lick him on his stupid face even though the dog must smell so bad now even Scrattymatty would take a step back and think about it. Anyway, me and Toto we were sort of standing there watching, but trying to look natural and cool so that nobody would notice or think twice about us, just fading into the scenery like good spies do - I mean a spy that wears flash clothes and is really beautiful would be so memorable and it doesn't make sense, which I guess is why James Bond is foney even though it's good to watch on bank holidays and stuff though not as good as *The Saint* - the old one with Ian Ogilvy and then that even isn't as good as *Austin Powers* which is well cool and he knows Madonna and stuff cos he was in her video, although so was Ali-G and he's crap, but that ain't Austin Powers fault.

Where was I? Oh yeah, anyway, Matty kind of mustn't have remembered what he was meant to be doing or anything, so he got a bit of paper out of his pocket and even though I couldn't see it I just *knew* it was our ransom note, and he started reading it - there on Ms Courtney's driveway right outside her front door. Man, he must be *sooo* dumb, me and Toto were laughing but still trying to be cool, but it was so funny and Toto kept saying 'Can you see if his lips are moving', cos he reckons Matthews is so dumb he can't just read in his head and has to say the words as if he's still in primary school or something. Anyway, I was in English for a while with Matthews, and Toto is right - he *is* dumb, so his lips probably were moving.

Anyway, Matthews must have got to the bit where it said he should ring the bell and run and find the next note - which we'd stuck on a tree with Toto's nail gun around the corner - and he went around to the tree and we couldn't see him no more, but it didn't matter cos he came back down the driveway in a couple of minutes and he was holding an envelope, so we knew he'd found it and everything. No-one answered the door though, so I guess Ms Courtney must've been out, but it doesn't matter cos I can't imagine anyone is going to steal the dog shit – right – doh!

Anyway, I meant to say - the new note is where we step things up and start to make Matty look really dumb, well dumber, you know? Someone is bound to have seen him dumping a dog turd on Ms Courtney's step, but it might take a while for them to track him down and all, so we want something that is gonna get him good.

See ya!

Doctor Mooze

Tuesday 7th January

Man, today was real good fun again. Me and Toto, we decided to skip school and go up Cribbs and hang out. It was Toto's idea, cos he'd been talking to Minto who always dresses real cool and Toto really liked his sunglasses which are Oakley and well cool and over £100 a pair. You don't even get a naff granny-glasses case with them or anything with one of those sad bits of cloth for polishing the lenses and all - no you get this wicked little black bag which is made of the cloth stuff for polishing the glasses, and it's got this wicked sort of drawstring on it to keep your glasses in the bag. They're *sooo* wicked and Toto's been going on about them for ages and Minto finally told him about this really cool skate-boarder shop where you can get all the coolest Oakleys and Quiksilver hoodies and Bill-a-Bong shirts and surfer shorts and Vans and Fly trainers and they sell skateboards and snowboards as well.

Anyway, Minto told Toto this yesterday, so we cut school to go up there and have a look to see if we can steal some sunglasses cos Toto's spent all his money on fags again and never had £100 anyway.

Yesterday I forgot to show you the note we left for Matthews on the tree after he'd done his turd delivery to Ms Courtney's house and all, so here it is:

To See Your Mutt Again
Go To School In A
Dress and Sing Hit
Me Baby One More
Time in the middle
of the football match in
the playground. Then go
to your locker and you
will find out where
your dog is

The song was my idea and Toto wasn't real sure about putting the footie match, in case there wasn't one or something, but Minto and his mates *always* play football and they're the coolest people in the school and they're the ones that will really rag on Matthews and make him suffer and everyone in the school and all Kate's friends will know what a dorky dweeb Matthews is. Man I can't wait.

Anyway, we went to Cribbs and found the shop, but it was really small and even though they did have glasses and stuff there were loads of assistants and they were really watching us even when I pretended to have a real bad cough so that they'd look at me and not Toto, so that he could really quickly grab some glasses. Well, even then they still watched Toto as well as me and I went red and stuff and I think it all sounded so foney that they *knew* what we were doing and this big man with dreads who looked really *coool*, looked really *angry* as well and said that he thought we should leave, so we did.

Anyway, we wandered around and Toto stole some Armani glasses from the Sunglasses shop on the first floor, which he's going to try and swap with Minto cos they cost £139.99, even if they aren't *sooo* cool (I don't think Minto will swap, cos if he'd wanted Armani he'd've like stole them himself). We also stole some books on computers from Waterstones, some sandwiches from Boots, a glass that Toto's girlie liked in John Lewis's - which is made from really heavy blue glass and looks old-fashioned, and she'll probably just leave it in a box on top of her wardrobe, like Mum does with everything Dad buys her and all - oh and we also got a little digital camera that clips on to Toto's mobile fone - but when we got back we realised that it was a dummy one they have in the shop so you can see what they look like, but don't matter if people steal them (I thought it was funny, cos we got chased when Toto grabbed that one and he thought he was Joe Cool all the way home in Minto's car, and was being really foney and bragging and trying to impress everyone.)

Yeah, I forgot that - we met Minto who was also skipping school in the car park and he'd hot-wired this old BMW and was going to go and race it to Weston, but said it was cool if we wanted a lift home first. Minto is real cool like that, he does really cool things but never ever boasts about them like Toto or acts all foney, you know? He just does them and if we hadn't seen him he'd never have mentioned it or anything. He really does make Toto look a real foney little boy with all his lies and blagging and foney boasting and stuff - but he does make me laugh. Minto told me that when I'm a bit older he'll show me how to steal cars too - though I think he forgot that it tells you how to do it in that book he gave me which is *sooo* cool and I keep reading it and stuff. He was funny too, cos all he kept saying was 'I got dem Black Man's Wheels, Yesirree', over and over in this really foney American sort of slave voice, and then laughing like the Voodoo man in *Live and Let Die*.

Anyway, I'm going to spy on Mattyman now, so I'll write more later if anything good happens

Doctor Mooze

Later

OK, so this day has just got better and better - man it's *sooo* very cool. *Sooo* fucking *A* man. *Sooo* cool.

See, Toto's plan - it worked. I mean, I guess I didn't think it really would. It all sounded so *easy* and I know we could see Scrattyboy and everything, but I never thought we could pull the whole thing off. We sat down to see what Matthews was up to and to be honest I was like - yaaawn - do we haaave to? The idea of watching Fattymatty jacking off was appealing - like *not.*

But anyway, it was OK, cos as soon as we connected to Matthews' computer, Toto turned on the webcam again and there was Mr Matthews using their it. I jumped and stuff, cos we haven't seen him before and then I was scared that he'd notice that we'd changed our Dad's bill and that he'd undercharged him and then he'd stroke his chin like he was thinking about it - then point at me and say that he knew exactly how we'd done it and that he was coming round to our house to tell my Dad and then Matthews would tell Kate and everyone would know that we were scrattier than Matthews. But he didn't, and Toto put the webcam picture in a small window so we could see what Mr Matthews was doing and he was on the net and my heart just went pop.

Everything seemed to stop, and it was like when everything goes all *slow-mo* in the Matrix and all and Keeney Reeves just hangs in the air and the picture moves round him - I guess the camera moved round him really - and I looked at Toto and he was turning to me and we both started to lift our hands and at the same time as we high-five'd everything suddenly went quick again. Toto grabbed the mouse just as I was grabbing the mouse and it fell on the floor, except it never got that far cos it's got a lead on it cos the cordless one is shit and Toto started pulling the mouse up on to the desk as quick as he could and I was trying to get out of the way and falling off my chair and before I hit the floor Toto managed to move the mouse and click on the record button, just as Mr Matthews hit the OK button on the payment page on *Amazon*.

And we'd done it. We'd managed to record Mr Matthews putting all his credit card details into the *Amazon* page and now we had them and now we had him, after waiting all this time and hoping that one day he'd actually buy something online and that we'd be lucky and get him and we had and we have. We've got the bastard. We've got the scratty piece of shit and now we're going to make him suffer now we're going to make them all pay. Me and Toto just sat there for a while and then Toto ran the recording to make sure it was still there (it was) and printed it in full screen mode so we had it all even if the computer blew up or anything.

Doctor Mooze

Even Later

Hi Again! Man we've had a cool time since I wrote the last bit. See, I didn't realise that Toto had got this all so planned out. He'd told me his master plan in a real *quiet* voice late at night and all, but I think I must have got bored or fed-up of him being a foney or fallen asleep but he had a really cool plan and it's *sooo* dark. I'm a bit scared that we might get caught, cos it all seems a lot more serious and everything, but Toto has been *sooo* right this far that I guess I better trust him. This bit has been real fun, cos now we've got Mr Scrattymatty's credit card numbers and *hotmail* account and everything so we can do what we want.

Anyway, the first part of Toto's plan was to buy loads of really stupid stuff and have it delivered to the scratty house, I mean it's all really useful things they need like air fresheners and cleaning stuff like Mr Sheen and deodorants and stuff, but then he started looking for dog blankets and Minced Morcels and Winalot, and we found that you can get all this stuff delivered by Tesco and Sainsburys and the Co-Op and all these different supermarkets - so that's what we did - we ordered every cleaning thing they all had. We've sent him 300 packs of Surf and 250 Magic Tree air-fresheners and 1000 Haze aerosol cans of air-freshener and so much Domestos and Harpic and Sure for Women and Mum deodorant and stuff and we've asked that they all get delivered on the same day, so we can hang around or go and call on Matthews and pretend to be his friend just so we're there when everything turns up - which I thought was *sooo* cool.

Anyway, I thought that was going to be it, but Toto's got loads of plans and ideas that are really nasty and I'm glad he's my brother and not my enemy, cos I think he's really good at being bad.

Well, when we got bored ordering all the cleaning stuff and

dog stuff, Toto decided that we should waste loads of Mr Matthews' money, so we logged on to *bet365* - which is a place you can place bets and stuff, and had really stupid bets for loads of money. I mean, we bet £2000 that Man United would lose 10-nil, and £1000 that West Brom. would win the premiership and £500 that Arsenal would be relegated - stuff like that. Then we decided to book a holiday in Iran for Matthews' Mum and Dad, which cost another £1500 or something like that anyway.

Anyway, once we'd done all that I was getting a bit bored. It was funny that we'd wasted all Scratdad's money and all, but it was on a credit card and he'd get it all back anyway if he complained and stuff cos they say so in all the adverts. Don't get me wrong, it was all really good fun and stuff, but …

Anyway, I said to Toto that I was going to go and watch TV or something or maybe play *WWE*, but he started saying 'No you gotta stay, you gotta stay' and I'm like, 'But this is boring man, this is like *sooo* tired' and he just kind of laughed and said that we were just coming to the best part. We were just getting to the bit where we really take our revenge and make Matty and his Dad suffer the mostest.

Anyway, I shrugged a bit cos I couldn't see what else we could do. But, like I say, Toto has been *sooo* right about this and it's really funny to think of what the family scratty will feel like when that bill comes for their card and stuff.

Anyway, Toto got all mysterious and checked outside the room – like Matty did when he was looking at his Page 3s and stuff - only this time Toto was making sure that my Mum and Dad were *not* creeping up on us like Japanese soldiers in the war in Viet Nam who are trying to find Rambo or someone so that they can put him in a pit and play cards with him and then make him play Russian Roulette which is a game you play with a gun where you're meant to shoot yourself – which is really dumb, even for a movie, but I guess they were really bored in them days cos they never even had the internet or Sky or anything.

Anyway, I guess my Mum and Dad *weren't* crawling up the stairs and along the landing or anything, so Toto settled down a bit and sat in front of the computer, then shut down BackOrifice. Next he opened Internet Explorer and got a bit of paper out of his pocket which had loads of URLs on it, and then he turned to me and looked really serious and just stared, like he was some nut-job or mental home person or something. Then it was like he'd made a really hard decision and sort of sat up a bit and started speaking quite quietly, not like he was scared that somebody would hear or anything, more like he wanted to tell me how it was and wanted to make sure that I understood and all.

'Panton', he started, which was weird cos he usually calls me Shithead or Li'l Bro or something,

'Do you remember why it was that we started all of this?' – I just nodded and wondered why he was asking and all, but he was so serious I didn't interrupt or nothing.

Then he said, 'See, I really, really like Becky, and you really, really like Kate, but we've got a problem. *Matthews*. See, Becky is getting really fed-up of Kate coming home and smelling of dog piss. Getting rid of the dog helped, but the smell just hangs around don't it?'

I nodded again. 'So that's my problem, I've got to protect *my woman*.'

He stood up and started walking around the room, like a teacher or something.

'*Your* problem Panton, is that you never had the guts to ask Kate out or asked her to be your girlfriend, cos you were never sure that you really liked her, until, that is, you saw her with Matthews'.

I really wanted to hit him now, cos I have *always* liked Kate, but I just didn't know what to do – I mean, how would I know – doh! *He's* the older brother and everything and I don't reckon he knows anything really, but he continued and I figured I could hit him afterwards.

'So *that* was it, Panton – Matthews really pissed us both off and we've really stiffed him. We've really done a number on him and now on his Dad. But what I want to know is whether you have got the guts to go this one last step? Have you got the bottle to really finish this once and for all, so Kate will never want to see Matty again and you can ask her out and she'll be your girlfriend and I can cop a feel without Becky whinging about her sister smelling of dog piss?'.

He stopped talking then and I was sure that he wanted me to say something, but I'd got a bit lost in the middle and I must admit a bit bored and I'd started to think of Kate and then of The Rock getting smacked down by The Undertaker and thrown into the crowd and hit with a tombstone or something. But he was waiting, so I asked him what he wanted me to do. He smiled a bit now, cos I think he knew we were both still on the same side and that we were still family and that I wouldn't rat him out or grass him up or blow the whistle or leave him in the lurch or anything like that.

'Cool, Panton. Now all we've got to do is register for a few websites, like when we set up *Geocities* and stuff.'

That sounded pretty easy to me and I just said 'cool!'. But he hadn't finished and said 'Yeah, it's cool – just this time we're going to be using Mr Matthews' name and credit card instead of just making one up'.

OK – it didn't sound loads more interesting but it was a bit different if nothing else, so Toto read out the URLs and I typed them in and we registered Mr Matty on some weird sites called *minor-69er.com; boytoys.cl; xxxbritneynakid.com* and *wikidpixxxx.fr*

See ya!

Doctor Mooze

Wednesday 8th January

OK. I've said a lot of things since I've been writing this blog or diary or whatever it is and I guess you know that I'm not Matthews' biggest fan and really don't think he's worthy of being Kate's boyfriend. But I've been worrying about whether me and Toto's plan has got a bit heavy and a bit too cruel. I felt bad when we took their dog and Toto threw it on the railway track and the train was coming and we could see it coming and I thought Toto was only fooling and that we'd just take it far from Matthews' house and let it go or something, cos it was *sooo* dumb that there was no way it would ever find its way back to their shitty house. They hadn't had it long or anything so I mean they couldn't have even liked it that much, could they?

I've been thinking that maybe they do and I'm not sure that we did the right thing, even if it was funny. It's like Mr Matty's credit card and that. It's been fun hanging around and stuff waiting for our plan to come together - but when we finally got his credit card and that, it was fun to order all that crap and stuff but it soon got really boring. I mean I was really not sleeping too good the last couple of nights and worrying that we might get caught - that someone would suss that we sent Matthews those ransom notes, or someone would find his shitty dead dog or maybe Mr Matty would find BackOrifice on his computer and work out that I'd put it on there or maybe even Matthews and Kate would get engaged or Kate would get pregnant or something cos she's been going all the way with the fat greasy slimy bastard and I keep waking up all hot and wet and all I can see is Matthews kissing Kate or his dead dog trailing after me when I'm walking back from school and even though I start running and he's going really, really slow, he's still catching me up like in the movies, even though he's a zombie dog and the train cut off two of his legs and he screamed like a kid that's really hurt itself and screamed and screamed and kept whining and there was so much blood - I mean how the fuck does one dog have so much fucking blood?

It was only a titchy little dog and its blood seemed to go everywhere and it was whining and screaming like the pigs in Hannibal and all when they're ripping that bloke to pieces and the nutter geezer is doing that funny thing with his mouth everyone did after Silence of the Lambs came out on DVD and Sky, and all the time the blood kept pouring out of it's neck and stumpy legs.

Toto got worried that someone would hear it and we'd get caught, so we tried to make it go quiet by saying 'Shh!' and stroking its head and patting it and saying 'Good dog!' and all the time it was screaming and crying, and trying to bite us. I didn't know that dogs could cry with real tears. I never saw a dog cry, but Matthews' dog had these big tears running down its face and it was looking at me and crying.

I was going 'Shh!' but it must have been in so much pain, and it was crying so much and just looking at me all confused, like it wanted to say 'I'm only a titchy little dog - why the fuck did you do this to me? Why did you have a go at me when I never did nothing to you?' and I'm looking at its eyes and it's crying and I feel bad. I felt so bad and then Toto is saying 'We got to shut it up Panton, we got to make it go quiet' and I'm saying 'Shh, doggie, Shh!' and trying to pat it, but I can't find a big enough space that's not covered in blood and shit - cos it had shat itself, you know? All the time these tears are running down its face and it's crying so loud so loud and whining and crying - and then it stopped. And I couldn't see the tears no more.

It went so quiet and all I could hear was Toto's breathing. And all I could see was blood and grey jelly, and there were bits of grey jelly on my jeans and I look down and I can't work out where the grey jelly has come from and I don't know why it has got so quiet all of a sudden and I look at Toto and want to ask him where the jelly has come from and where the noise and tears are and I look at Toto and he's still holding the brick, still holding the brick in his hand and the jelly is on the brick and there's blood on the brick and then I know that Toto has made the dog go quiet and I know that it don't hurt no more and I know that Toto has just smashed the doggie's brains in.

God I hate dreams like that, but I guess it's cos I haven't been sure about what we're doing and it nags, nags, nags at the back of my head and it makes it hurt and then I think about: Should we just stop? Should we just tell Matthews to forget it and tell him where to find his dog - not really tell him, I mean I don't want to get into trouble and we'd get serious shit for all this. No, I mean we could send another note or something. But then I think of Kate again and even though Dad always says that there are loads more fish in the sea, she's the only fish I want.

But for days I've just been thinking that maybe we should give up on our revenge and that maybe we're going a bit over the top and I've said it to Toto, but he loves it man, you know what I mean, he really likes all this sneaky stuff cos I guess it's not foney, and everything he ever does is all bullshit and foney and full of hot air and maybe this is something real, and I look at him and then start worrying too cos I can't see him keeping his mouth shut, cos he *sooo* loves being the man, you know, and he always gives it large when he talks about things he's made up and I really can't see him keeping it quiet when there's something real to talk about.

So that's it, I wanted to tell you that I've been having my *worries* about all this and getting scared and not really enjoying it or trusting Toto or thinking it's been worth it and everything. I wanted you to know that when I woke up this morning, that was exactly how I felt. I could have given it all up and just played footie and stuff, no problem. I wanted you to know this, so that when I talk about today you'll see it was really unexpected and really a big surprise.

Cos, I want to tell you that today, has been the **BEST FUCKING DAY OF MY LIFE.** I have never, ever, enjoyed a day like I enjoyed today. I've never gone to school and just wished that the day would never end, I so wanted to just talk and laff with people that I never even played footie or nothing, cos today has been the **PERFECT DAY**. Today has been the day that I will tell my friends and grandchildren about when they ask 'What was the best day you ever had Grandad Panton' and if I'm ever in a pub and got interviewed cos the BBC are doing one of their real dumb survey things, and I'm 18 and drinking cider and wearing a Ben Sherman shirt and desert boots and maybe Armani jeans or Nu-Gear cargoes or something, and an interviewer says 'Can I ask you a few questions for our survey on what everyone in the country thinks about things, so the future people of England will have a record like that Magna Carta thing that Robin Hood did and all' and if someone asked me I'd said 'Yeah' and then if they said, 'What was the best fucking day you ever had?' I'd wait a second and pretend to think about it, even though I wouldn't need to think about it cos I'd know already and I'd scratch my head or rub my chin or something and take a sip of my cider and then say 'Well,' and pause a minute and maybe scratch my head or rub my chin again, and then I'd say 'Well, it's got to be that day when I was ten or maybe eleven, when that bloke Matthews came into school and stood in the middle of a football game that my best mate Minto and me and a few other blokes were playing in and started to sing a song' and I can imagine the BBC person saying 'So Mr Panton, what happened next' and I'd just look him straight in the eye and take another sip of my cider or vodka and Red Bull or something, and stretch a little as the whole country just waited for me to answer him, then slowly I'd say, 'Well, everything went mad and everybody started laughing, cos the thing I didn't mention before was that he was wearing a dress he'd robbed off the lady who later became my wife. But we didn't know that then cos all we could see was this fat smelly greasy little shit called Matthews standing in the middle of the playground, wearing this really flowery dress that was loads too small for him, him being a fat blubber belly and all, and then he started to sing a Britney Spears song that was popular back then, but cheesy now, but she was a really big singer then and all.'

Then I'd have another sip of my cider and the guy, who'd be stunned by this, and the whole nation would be wondering what the song was, and the interviewer who'd probably over-run by miles cos I'd been so cool, and hadn't gone back to the studio cos this would be *sooo* big, and why he'd become a journalist in the first place and everything. Well, this geezer would finally pull himself together and ask 'So, I think I speak for the nation when I ask - what was the song he was singing?' - and I'd just smirk and feel the tension as people - grannies, kids, and Mums and Dads and everyone - lean forward toward the telly so that they can hear my answer and I take another sip of my cider before I answer and eventually smile and say 'Oh, the song he sang was "Hit Me Baby One more Time".' And I can imagine that the interviewer would be nearly wetting himself by then and would have to take deep breaths and be imagining winning one of those wank TV awards people give to each other at hotels in London and places, and then he'd say 'But what happened next?' and then I'd definitely smirk, and maybe have a smug smile and I would just say 'Oh, then the whole school kicked the shit out of him'.

Oh man, it was *sooo cool.* But that wasn't it, I mean yeah once he turned up and sang his song, I just thought there is *nooo way* on earth this could get better. I mean all the kids in our class were there - all of Minto's friends, Minto, Kate and all her friends - and it was *sooo* funny. I could feel my sides splitting. Everyone all over the playground just stopped and watched him walk across the playground in his little poxy flowery dress and stop in the middle and people began wolf-whistling him and laughing and all the time I could see that he was crying and really blarting like a girl and I could see that he'd got our ransom note in one of his hands and another bit of paper in the other and I didn't know what that was at first until he cleared his throat and coughed a bit and sort of sobbed and then started singing. He was reading from this other bit of paper that wasn't our ransom note - and when he started singing everyone sort of went quiet so that they could hear him and he'd only been singing a bit when everyone realised what the song was and started laughing again and then I saw Kate and she was sort of white and I think she must have realised that he was wearing her dress cos then she went really red and burst into tears, cos I guess everyone knows that he's meant to be her boyfriend - cos Matthews told everyone that anyway. And then Kate sort of turned away and started running out of the school playground and out the gates and then round a corner so I couldn't see her no more.

Anyway, I thought I should go after Kate and see if she's alright, but then Minto's friends who he'd been playing football with had started getting closer to Matthews and pulling his hair and calling him Girlie and poof and Matilda and stuff and pushing him around and then someone knelt behind him, and he's still singing and reading the words from this bit of paper and all, and then someone just pushed him a little bit so he took a little step back, but fell over the boy that had knelt behind him and

Matthews kind of fell over backwards really slowly and his legs went in the air and I couldn't see but I think it was Minto who pushed him cos he was closest and he shouted 'He hasn't got his knickers on' and everybody surged forward to see, I guess, though I really didn't want to after the webcam thing with the Page 3 pictures and everything so I never. But then people must have started giving Matthews digs, cos he was on the floor and couldn't do much and people do it when they think you can't hit them back don't they?

Anyway, everybody's having a riot and Matthews is kind of disappearing beneath all these people running across and trying to kick him and then Ms Courtney came into the playground and blew her whistle and everybody sort of stopped and you're meant to stand still, but everyone was trying to drift away and she blew her whistle again and shouted 'Nobody move' and nobody did move cos Ms Courtney's scary when she's angry and she looked angry then.

I forgot to say that in Assembly this morning the Headmistress, Mrs Blake, said something about if anybody knows anything about certain 'articles' being delivered to the home of one of our teachers, then they should come and see her and I saw Matthews look across at Ms Courtney even though Mrs Blake hadn't said it was her and he's so dumb cos he could only know to look at Ms Courtney if he was involved - doh! and I could see from the corner of my eye that Ms Courtney noticed that he'd looked and everyone must have noticed that he'd gone bright red and all cos I could see him glowing, man - he was like a beetroot or a radish or something.

Anyway, at the end of the assembly Ms Courtney was coming across to our class. We stand near the back, you know? But Matthews went out the other door real quick and you could see that Ms Courtney wanted to shout after him but the Head was reading Notices and she left it cos I guess she thought she'd get him later. Except in Science, which was our first lesson, Ms Courtney came in and asked to see Matthews, but he'd wagged the lesson and she looked well angry when Mr Rockwood, our teacher, said he wasn't there.

But anyway, when she came into the playground she made straight for the middle of the fight and everybody sort of parted and moved to one side so that there was a ring of people around Matthews, who was lying on the floor with his dress ripped and covered in shit and dirt and blood running down his face and crying like the girl he looked. Man, it was really funny and I felt really pleased inside and not sorry for him or anything cos he's *sooo* an asshole and he's beneath my respect and a non-person of the lowest order, or even less.

Anyway, Ms Courtney stood over him for a second and told him to get up and then told everyone else to go away and back to class, and Matthews I think pretended that he couldn't get up and Ms Courtney started telling him that he was going to be expelled for this if he didn't get up straight away and eventually he got up and he was still holding his bits of paper and Ms Courtney asked him what they were and he handed one over and she read it and sort of said 'Britney Spears - who the hell is Britney Spears?' and he said something and gave her the other bit of paper - which must have been our ransom note and she read it and said something quietly to him and he said something back that I couldn't hear. And then she ripped up the ransom note and said really loudly 'If you think this pathetic attempt to get you off the hook for delivering a pile of rubbish to my house will work, you've got another think coming' and Matthews started crying again and she said 'Come with me. We're going to ring your parents and see what they have to say' and Matthews looked really panicked and I guess he was thinking that he'd done his part of the bargain and now he wanted to know how to get his dog back and I could see him all of a sudden look really determined and he pulled his arm away from Ms Courtney, who was only holding it really lightly, and she looked really shocked and then he legged it across the playground and into the school towards the lockers.

Anyway, I looked at Minto and pointed at the other door with my eyebrows and we both nipped into the school that way and ran to the lockers the long route. Anyway, when we got there Matthews was already trying to open his locker but the key wouldn't work and that was when Toto walked up behind me and Minto and said 'Looks like that locker has been superglued doesn't it?' and me and Minto just fell about you know, cos Toto was juggling this tube of glue and it were *sooo* obvious that he'd done it, but no-one knew except us. And then Ms Courtney must have caught up and she shouted at Matthews something like 'Don't you move' and he's being really desperate and trying to open his locker and she got to him and slapped him round the head and he was saying 'I've got to open my locker' and 'I gotta get my dog back' and she was telling him to shut-up and she hit him again and then another voice shouted 'Ms Courtney! What on earth do you think you're doing' and everyone went quiet, cos it was Mrs Blake and she's a really scary bitch and could have been a wookie, cos she's well hairy.

Anyway, Ms Courtney and Matthews and Mrs Blake all seemed to be having a conversation for ages and eventually Mrs Blake got one of the first years and he went and got the caretaker, which I guess is what she wanted, and then he came back with a crowbar or something and broke the lock on Matthews' locker and then all shit broke loose again and Matthews was crying and Ms Courtney was throwing up and Mrs Blake just looked white and the caretaker went and got a mop, cos I guess that's what caretakers do.

See, when me and Toto broke into the school the other day we decided that we would put the finishing touches to our plan for Scrattymatty. We could have had him trailing around for ever with our stupid clues and all, but we'd've got bored or he'd've just decided the dog weren't worth it or we'd've got caught or something, so we figured we wanted a big ending like on a movie or something where it all kind of leads up to the building blowing up and stuff. So when we broke in, we figured we'd need to make it hard for Matthews to get into his locker and stuff, cos we didn't want him to sneak in without anyone knowing - I didn't know Toto was going to glue it or anything, but I knew he was planning to do something.

Anyway, when Toto came up with the notes idea and then we decided to get Scratty to take stuff to Ms Courtney's house, Toto wanted to make sure that even if no-one saw Matthews delivering stuff to her house, that he'd still get caught you know?

So we wanted to make sure that when Matty managed to get his locker open he'd have a bit of an audience, and that we'd have made sure that his audience had something to look at that would finger him for the Courtney job, if you know what I mean.

So, when the caretaker opened Matty's locker, the first thing Mrs Blake and Ms Courtney and Matthews must have noticed was the smell. I was standing a bit far away to see and all, and they were all crowded around the locker so no-one could see their faces, but as they opened it Matty's dog must have fell out and I saw Matty take a step forward as though he was going to catch it cos it was jumping up at him so that it could lick his face and they'd all live happily ever after. But he started to step forward and then stopped and took a little step back. Then he just screamed - man he screamed - like a little girl. He screamed like his dog screamed when the train went over him, you know?

Ms Courtney stepped away from the locker with her hand to

her mouth and I could see she was going to throw up, and then she did - she heaved all over the floor and the caretaker's feet, and he jumped back and knocked over his mop bucket. I just *sooo* wanted to laugh, but Matthews was still screaming, you know, and his dog was on the floor now cos it had fallen out, and everyone could see that it didn't have any legs left (cos it was too big to get in the locker if we'd left the other two on, so Toto chopped them off). Then a girl screamed cos she could see that the dog didn't have any eyes or nothing cos we'd popped those out and replaced them with these big bubble gum eyes, that looked like real horror movie eyes, you know, and are bright red and have veins and stuff all over them, and the dog looked like it had been taken over by the devil and could see your soul and wanted to feed on your children's blood and stuff. I reckon that was what scared the girl anyway, cos we'd put lipstick on the dog, really thick and bright red, but that was just silly and not really scary.

Anyway, I could see Matthews hugging his dog and getting dried blood all over him, and it was scabs you know, and I just thought that scabby Matty was about right, you know? But Mrs Blake was looking at the rest of the stuff in the locker, cos we hadn't just put the dog in there.

First of all she took out the Dunkin Donuts box and looked inside and then jumped and dropped it - cos we'd put this really rank dog turd in there, cos we knew somebody would open it, you know? By now Ms Courtney had stopped puking and she said something to Mrs Blake and pointed at the donut box - I guess Ms Courtney was saying that she'd had donuts dumped at her house, or that she'd seen Matty looking at her in assembly or something.

Anyway, the next thing Mrs Blake took out was a rolled up paper, which we'd put a bit of old ribbon around so that it looked like a pirate's map or scroll or something, and when she opened it there was a really simple map that we'd traced that showed how to get to Ms Courtney's house - and Ms Courtney got really excited at this and probably really pissed off cos we'd put an arrow that pointed to her house and we'd written 'Old Slag' next to it and Toto had copied Matthews' writing and stuff, which is really plebby and easy to copy from one of his school books I swiped - but Toto still thought he was a master forger like the blind bloke in the Great Escape.

Anyway, the only other stuff that was in there was a letter we'd nicked from the front door of Ms Courtney's house and a picture of Ms Courtney's head that we'd put on the body of a pig in Photoshop and then printed out. I think Toto copied it on to Matthews' computer as well, just in case anybody ever had a look. So anyway, I decided to go cos you could see that Mrs Blake was really pissed off and all, and it was time for lessons and everything and I didn't want her to notice me hanging around too much.

Anyway, later on - after we'd gone to Chemistry and then Maths - one of the teachers told us that Matthews had been suspended cos of all the stuff he had in his locker and cos he'd admitted taking stuff to Ms Courtney's house and everything. Man, I couldn't believe it. I mean, they really thought that Matthews was stupid enough to do all that and keep the evidence in his locker (which he is) - but I can't believe that they think he'd really keep his dead dog in there as well! He's stupid, but why would he do that? Why would he keep his dead dog and put lippie on it and false chewing gum eyes?

Teachers really are so *lame* you know? I mean, we did all this but I didn't think anyone would think it was down to him, you know? We just wanted to torture him a bit.

Anyway, when I went home it was the only thing anyone was

talking about and everyone was saying that Matthews had got to go to the police and answer questions - which made me a bit scared, but Minto said that they wouldn't take him to the police just for having stuff in his locker and dropping a turd at a teachers house - unless he was black and carrying' or something - I think he meant drugs. So I didn't worry anymore cos we hadn't put any of them in there.

Doctor Mooze

Kate

Later:

Man this has been such a cool day, you know. I mean all the stuff at school was wicked and I think that Matthews really has been suspended. Which is funny and cool and stuff, but more importantly, Becky told Toto that Kate has dumped the scrattyone as well, which is everything I've been dreaming about for *sooo* long, you know, and Toto's being *sooo* funny, telling me to comb my hair and get across to Kate's house and give her a shoulder to cry on or something hard to bite on to. He's funny, talks crap, but makes me laugh anyway and it's all down to Toto that Kate has dumped Matthews and he's the town scratter and stuff and I love him like my own brother, which he is, cos he's the man.

Anyway, we've been on BackOrifice for one last time and we're putting the final part of the plan into action.

I mean, we've wiped out Matthews *soo* much already that I suppose we could just leave it now and pat ourselves on the back and let sleeping dogs die and everything, but, like Toto said, we've got a plan and we better stick to it cos if you don't tie up the loose ends things have a habit of coming unravelled (which I reckon I heard once in a film, but I ain't going to spoil things by calling him a foney again now, you know).

Anyway, as I said, we went on to BackOrifice and got on to *hotmail* with Matthews' *hotmail* account login and sent this email to *helpme @childline.org.uk*:

From: DJMatty[mailto:DJMATTY10776@hotmail.com]
Sent: Wednesday, January 08, 2003 10:47 PM
To: helpme@childline.org.uk
Subject: Help Me Please

Dear Sir or Madam
I really, really hope that you can help me because it's nearly eleven o'clock and my Dad will be back from the pub soon and he's already in a bad mood with me cos I got suspended from school today even though it wasn't my fault and I never killed our dog and put it in my locker and it must have been someone else, but I don't know who would do such a thing, because that's such a horrible thing to do and they would have to be really clever and I can't think who would do that.

But my Dad won't believe me and when he gets back from the pub he's always in such a bad mood and I know it's fault because he does everything for me and loves me and I know they're only games that all Dads play with their sons and that Mum wouldn't understand, but I don't like those games and if he's in a bad mood he's so rough, you know? And he hurts me sometimes and then doesn't talk to me for days and I just feel horrible and dirty because I don't like the games and that must spoil them for him and he does everything for me and my Mum and loves us all and I can't even do this one small thing for him, you know?

So please, if you can help me to do things right so that I don't force my Dad to hit me for my own good it would be really nice and I'd feel a lot happier

Thank you, Matthews XX

Even Later

I can't believe it. I can't believe the fucker would do this to me.I mean he's my brother and we've got blood and he's betrayed me, the foney fucking bastard. We've been through so fucking much together over the last few days and then the prick fuckin' betrays me like a piece of shit. We had a plan and I trusted him with my life and kept my mouth shut and helped him out and it was me that put BackOrifice and everything on Mattyman's computer, and kept my nerve, and all he fucking did was sit at home while me and Minto sorted everything out. All the time he planned to betray me - all the time he got me to betray myself and I know why.

That's the worst thing, I mean if it was anyone else and I didn't know them so well, I would still hate it. But if I didn't know why they were doing it at least I'd have something to wonder about, you know? But with this bastard Toto – my brother - I know exactly why he did it and it's just cos he's *sooo* fucking small, so fucking pitiful that he has to put me down all the time in case I end up being better at something than him – and he is *sooo* meant to be the older brother and better at everything.

But I can't believe the foney fucker's done it. I mean, we've spent *sooo* long trying to make Matty look the school scratter and the fucking nobody, and tried to make sure that everybody knows, which is the best bit cos that means Kate knows and she'll dump him – and we've done it. I mean we've fucking done it and I never really thought we could and didn't believe we could. But we finally did it, and Kate has dumped Scratty and I'm thinking that maybe she might like me again, you know? And then I find out that that foney fuck bastard brother of mine has betrayed me and now everyone will think I'm as shit as Matty. Everyone will think that I'm a loser too – and if people think it then it's true, cos if Kate believes it then she won't be my girlfriend, and if she knows it everybody will know it and then it's true – cos if everyone believes it, it really is true – cos that's what we done to Matty and now Toto's done the same to me.

When he told me I just sat there with my mouth open and all I could say was 'Why?' All I could think was *Betrayal.* And I guess the worst thing is that it was me who actually did it, the cunt got me to stitch myself up. I mean I will *never* forget this and I will *never* forgive him for this however long we live, cos he's my brother and he's betrayed me.

God, I can't believe I was so stupid, I mean when he took that picture of me when I got out of the fucking bath, I really believed him when he said that he'd deleted it – I mean, I didn't think for a minute that he'd have kept a copy, you know. I mean, he's my fucking brother - why would he want a picture of me with a hard-on? And all the time the prick, the *foney fuck*,had it all planned. He knew how he was going to try and stiff Mr Matty with the peedo game and everything - he knew that everybody would think that Matty had lost it cos of his old man playing his 'special games' with him – but I figured that would be enough – but not for Toto.

See, he wanted to make sure, so we did the online things and signed Mr Matty up to all those weird websites and we ordered him some magazines from Amsterdam and all, and I figured that that was that. Oh, but not fucking Toto - no he fucking wanted something closer to home than that – and that's the worst of it, he thinks I'm being *Mr Fuckin' Unreasonable* and funny cos I won't pretend that Mr Matty came on to me as well! I couldn't believe it when he said 'I've sent an email to chidline.org.uk from you as well Panton. All you have to do is say that Mr Matthews wanted to take your picture and you were scared, so you let him'.

I was *sooo* shocked I couldn't believe it, and all I could say was 'But there aren't any pictures – what good would it do without any pictures?' and he just laughed and told me how I'd copied the picture he'd taken of me getting out the bath on to Matty's computer when I put BackOrifice on there.

I just looked at him, and then I could feel this red cloud coming all over me, you know, and I just jumped at him and started hitting him and trying to smash the smug fucker's face, and all I wanted to do was kill him you know?

All I wanted to do was rip out his throat and scream into the hole that he'd killed me. He'd ruined everything, and didn't he realise just how bad this was? Didn't he realise that Kate wouldn't want to see me if she thought I was damaged goods – cos **I AM NO DIFFERENT TO MATTHEWS -** I'd be the same scum that he was. God I hate him, I really do hate him and I hope his nose really is broken, and I don't care if I have to stay in my room for fucking ever. He's no brother of mine. He's not my family. He's nothing.

Doctor Mooze

The Latest

I'm still so pissed off with Toto. This isn't something that will just go away, you know?

The Childline people and the police are coming tomorrow, and I'm going to have to pretend that Mr Matty really did take that picture and all cos otherwise I'll have to tell the truth and that's even worse. I really do hate Toto. I can't believe he did this to me. I know what we've done to Matthews and his Dad is dark, but you don't do things like this to your family - you don't like shit on your own doorstep, you know.

I mean, this is *sooo* winding me up now, so I rang Minto – which I never do in case he doesn't want to talk to me and *busies* me, you know – which would be horrible. But I was really pissed off and rang him, and he answered, which was really nice, and I told him what had happened and he doesn't really like Toto anyway and he was really not impressed, you know.

Anyway, he's going to meet me at the end of the road in a bit and we're going to hang out or something, you know. I'm going to sneak out, cos everyone's in bed and I can walk out without anyone knowing. I mean, I've done it before and stuff and no-one ever notices. I'm really not looking forward to tomorrow, though - I really don't want to talk to the police or anyone. Anyway, I'll catch you later, all right?

Doctor Mooze

Post Script

Wednesday 8th January is the final entry in Panton's diary.

That night Panton and Minto stole Mr Matthews' car and, while driving round Bristol City Centre at high speed, were chased by a police car and lost control on a corner at over 115 miles per hour.

Neither Panton nor Minto was wearing a seat belt. They were thrown through the windscreen and suffered serious injuries. Both were pronounced dead on arrival at the Bristol Royal Infirmary.

The day after the crash, Mr Matthews was arrested and charged with offences relating to the possession of child pornography.

His computer was confiscated. Photographs of Panton and a video of his son were found on the hard drive, both of which he was unable to explain.

Mr Matthews took his own life while on remand.

Only the discovery of this diary by Panton's father revealed the truth and established Mr Matthews' innocence.

Where are they now?

Following the arrest of his father Matthews left school.

Becky dumped Toto, who has since been expelled and is currently awaiting a social worker's report relating to his part in the torture of Matthews, his father and their dog.

Panton's mother now lives with Terry in Salford, and Mr di Villa has returned to Spain to live with his sister.

The Matthews' dog, Butch, got a Christian burial, which is odd, because it never was what you'd call a believer of fairy tales, *you know?*